I0522608

Season of Reckoning

This is a work of fiction. All of the characters, organizations, and events portrayed in this novel are either products of the author's imagination or are used fictionally.

Season of Reckoning
Copyright © 2022 by L. Lee Shaw

All rights reserved. No part of this book may be used or reproduced in any manner whatever without written permission except in the case of brief quotations embodied in critical articles ort reviews. For information address: Boho Books, 36179 S. Sawtell Road, Molalla, OR 97038.

ISBN: 978-0-9988455-8-6 (paperback)
       978-0-9988455-9-3 (ebook)

Printed in the United States of America

Boho Books paperback edition / May 2022

Also by L. Lee Shaw

Blood Will Tell...
Monster Child
Aging Out
Love Imperfect
Flunking Magic

Dedication

To women everywhere who resist the patriarchy.

Table of Contents

Chapter One

The women sat at the table, Bibles closed and shoved to the side now that study was over. Pam brought a fresh pot of coffee from the kitchen, offering refills as she made her way around. Sugar and cream passed back and forth amid teaspoons tinkling against cups. Setting a platter of cookies in the middle of the table, Pam sank down into her chair as she handed napkins off to the other women.For a few moments there was only the contented sounds of the sweets being devoured, washed down with sips of coffee.

Then, Mona, the group's most recent and fervent member, asked, "What's with those old ladies on the other side of town? When I get stuff from the deli, I try to share like Pastor Barnwell says we should, and they act like they can't even hear me."

Miss Kepler, the elderly spinster, reached a skeletal hand toward the cookie plate. "Oh, my dear, has no one told you? They are witches."

Mona's pale blue eyes looked like they were about to pop out of her head and her jaw practically hit the table. "There are witches in Totem?"

Pam cleared her throat in irritation. "Actually, they're just some antiquated feminists who are so last century. Very strange, but harmless. Pastor would be just as happy if you didn't waste your time with them. They're not the type of people he wants in the congregation."

Miss Kepler studied the nibbled edge of her cookie. "Whatever you say, dear," she murmured.

***

In a cabin partially hidden from the parking lot by storefronts, a chanting woman circled her hands over a steaming pot.

"Double, double toil and trouble;
Fire burn and caldron bubble.
Fillet of a fenny snake,
In the caldron boil and bake;
Eye of newt and toe of frog,
Wool of bat and tongue of dog,
Adder's fork and blind-worm's sting,
Lizard's leg and howlet's wing,
For a charm of powerful trouble,
Like a hell-broth boil and bubble.

Double, double toil and trouble;
Fire burn and caldron bubble.
Cool it with a baboon's blood,
Then the charm is firm and good."

Jan hip-checked her in order to open the oven door and slide a muffin pan inside. "Ophelia, just add the cumin, and put the lid back on before it cools too much. What's with the weird sister shit anyway?"

Dipping a measuring spoon into the spice jar, Ophelia shook its contents across the chicken chili, giving it a good stir with a wooden spoon before putting the lid back on the dutch oven and tossing both spoons in the sink.

Picking up her wineglass, she followed Jan back to the living room where Becca and Felicity were sitting on the floor carefully winding strings of twinkle lights around squares of cardboard and placing them in a plastic tote. "Somebody make a note we need to replace that string of lights that went bad."

"I have a couple somewhere in my shop decorations if nobody remembers," Jan said. She pointed to a second tote. "Have the batteries been removed from the candles yet?"

Becca shook her head. "Nope."

Picking up the tote, Jan set it on the couch, tugging at its lid. "By the way, Ophelia just cursed the chili. However, I don't think any of it splattered over onto the cornbread."

"If you didn't want what we planned for dinner, you just had to say so," Felicity said. "Doing in the rest of us will leave you a little short-handed in the future."

Ophelia sipped from her glass. "Actually, it was just a dash of Shakespeare. And speaking of curses, I might as well share the bad news."

The other three women looked sharply at her.

"What bad news?" Becca asked warily.

"According to the quarterly chart I cast last night, a bad moon is set to rise, an ill-wind is gonna blow, and a shit storm is heading this direction."

"For real?" Jan asked, raising a skeptical eyebrow. She was well familiar with Ophelia's flair for the dramatic.

"For real. All stars are pointing to some heavy-duty crap landing on our doorsteps. Which, by the way, the tarot confirmed. Girls, Summerland is right in the crosshairs of some grand karmic event."

"Great. Something to look forward to," Felicity muttered.

"Why is it never rainbows, unicorns, and pots of gold?" Becca moaned.

"I can't control what's in the stars or cards. I just chart and lay out," Ophelia grumbled defensively.

"Well, since our own Queen of Darkness is prognosticating that soon there's gonna be rain all over our parade, obviously there is only one thing to do," Jan said.

Becca glanced at her. "Start casting every protection spell we know?"

"Hang amulets everywhere?" Felicity suggested.

Jan shook her head. "Lay in more wine. A lot more wine," she replied, holding up an opened bottle.

"Blessed be," the women answered as they held out their glasses.

***

Breathing shallowly to stave off another bout of coughing, the man switched his wipers from full-on to intermittent as the squall he had driven though gave way to just misty moisture settling on the minivan's windshield.

Pushing himself into the seat trying to relieve the pain between his shoulder blades, Evan Hjort unconsciously drew in a deep breath, triggering the cough that had plagued him for nearly a week. Every muscle in his chest felt like it was being torn apart, fiber by fiber, as he struggled to stifle the relentless tickle at the back of his throat. Fighting for breath, streaks of black began to cross his vision. He needed to get off the road before he wrecked the van. It wasn't much, but it was pretty much all he had left in the world, serving as both transportation and living quarters.

He missed the name of the town he was pulling into, caught as he was in a paroxysm of coughing. It didn't matter as long as he could get off the road. His headlights picked up a long building on the left-hand side, and the wide graveled area in front of it. He swung the van into it, gratefully cutting the engine before collapsing in on himself as his lungs threatened to explode.

A squat man in a yellow rain slicker carefully approached the poorly parked van. He glanced at the storefronts arrayed along the wooden sidewalk. There were no signs that any of the ladies were there. Creeping up to the door, he peeked through the driver side window. Security lights perched along the building's overhang illuminated a man lying back in the reclined driver's seat.

He gently tapped his fingertips on the window. The man turned his head before another bout of deep coughing hunched him forward in the seat.

Carefully observing for a moment, Enoch turned and scuttled across the parking lot. Rounding the end of the building, he paused and looked for the lighted rose-colored candle. He spotted it in Miss Jan's window. He trotted up the graveled tiers serving as stairs to the front door. Pushing back the hood on his slicker, he knocked diffidently. It was Miss Felicity who opened the door.

"Enoch?"

He pointed back to the parking lot. "Him sick."

Felicity stepped out the door and looked in the direction Enoch was pointing. "Who's sick?

The man looked down at his feet and shrugged. "Dunno. Man in… in…" Putting his hands up, he made a motion like he was steering a car.

"There's a man in a car who's sick?"

Enoch's head bobbed up and down. "Sick. Maybe sure."

Felicity reached out and squeezed him arm. "Let me get my jacket." Turning back to pull it off the coat tree, she answered the question on the face of the three other women. "Enoch says we have a sick man in the parking lot."

There was a clattering of wine glasses being set down as Jan, Becca, and Ophelia scrambled to their feet. In moments, they were all trotting towards the parking lot.

It was hard to determine the color of the minivan under the halogen lights and, at first, it appeared to be empty. It was only when they were actually beside the van that they were able to see its occupant. Felicity knocked on the window.

The man pulled himself up with the aid of the steering wheel. He turned the key enough to activate the electric window, rolling it down.

"I'm sorry if I shouldn't be parking here. I just needed to get off the road for a few minutes." His voice had the thick, wheezy sound of someone in the grip of heavy chest congestion.

"You're sick," Felicity said matter-of-factly.

He nodded, failing to muffle another coughing spell. Finally, he was able to speak. "I'm sorry. I can move if you want me to."

"Are you expected anyplace? Anyone we should call?"

He shook his head.

Felicity looked over his shoulder into the back of the van. There was a sleeping bag neatly spread over one side of the folded-down seats. Some shirts hung on a coat hook. There were a couple of duffle bags and a garbage bag that looked like it was also stuffed with clothes.

"Is this where you live?" she asked.

"For the moment." The rasp in his voice didn't muffle the shame.

"Well, you're not going to get over your crud living in there," Felicity said briskly. "We have a place you can stay until you are back on your feet." Turning toward the rest of them, she proposed, "The Crone, I think."

The other three women nodded. "Definitely," Becca said as she reached for a carabiner attached to the belt loop of her jeans. She handed it off to Jan, who immediately turned and headed towards a gravel path leading down from the parking lot.

"Enoch, hon, would you mind turning on the lights?"

Obediently, the man who had been watching from behind the women hurried in the direction of a box attached to the building. He opened it and carefully flipped the switch. The path became illuminated by a series of ground-level lights revealing the fronts of three small cabins arrayed along its edge. At the last of them, Jan unlocked the door, reaching around the jamb to turn on the inside and outside lights.

Felicity opened the van door. "Do you think you can make the walk?"

"Please. I really don't want to trouble you. I just needed to rest and catch my breath," Evan protested weakly. He reached for the ignition key.

Becca reached past Felicity and grasped Evan's arm, urging him out of the seat. "We have a philosophy here. When someone in need lands in our parking lot, we answer. You, sir, are in need."

There was no fight left in him, He had used it up long before the cold settled in his chest. He nodded and swung out of the car. He had no idea what this band of grey-haired women was about, but if they planned to kill him, he wasn't convinced it would be a bad thing.

Ophelia and Becca took up position on either side of him, guiding him toward the light spilling out of the cabin's open doorway.

"I'll get the stuff," Felicity said as she headed opposite in the direction of the larger cabins.

Upon reaching the little cabin, Becca placed a steadying hand on the man's back as they climbed the steps. He stopped inside, wavering a little on his feet. "How much does it cost? I'm not very flush right now." That was an understatement. A meal at a fast food place would just about break what was left of his bank.

"These are dedicated for those who need a temporary bit of shelter from life. We don't charge for them," Ophelia said.

Looking around, Evan realized that although it was quite small, it was, in fact, complete. The room he stood in contained a small, overstuffed loveseat, and an end table with a lamp. Just beyond the end of the couch was a miniscule kitchen area with a tiny sink, microwave, dorm-size refrigerator, and a couple of narrow cupboards above. A twin bed, already made up, could be seen through a doorway. He assumed there was a bathroom not visible from where he was standing. The red glow of a wall heater emitted welcome heat.

Becca held out her hand. "Hi, I'm Becca Calhoun. This Is Ophelia Swanner and Jan Dressler. If you would give me your keys, I will move your van to a more discreet location. Even in teeny, tiny Totem we still have our share of problems."

He lifted his hand and realized it was empty. A flash of bewilderment crossed his face. Becca patted him on the arm. "They are probably still in the van since we kinda hustled you out of it." She disappeared out the door.

"Let me give you a quick tour," Jan said. She showed him that the kitchen was complete with dishes, cookware, and a coffeemaker; the bathroom was stocked with towels and a shelf of personal necessities; and extra pillows and quilts were in the chest at the foot of the twin bed.

Felicity came through the door bearing a small tote. In short order, the women had emptied it as they set up an aromatherapy diffuser on the nightstand, administered herbal cough syrup, placed containers of lemon water, homemade chicken broth, and tea in the refrigerator.

"We hope you are able to sleep well," one of the women said as they moved to the door.

Evan looked at them. "You don't even know my name."

An odd look passed between them. Becca spoke. "You're welcome to give us your name or not as is comfortable for you."

"Evan. Evan Hjort," he said.

"Then goodnight, Mr. Hjort. Again, sleep well." The four women vanished out the door, closing it behind them.

There was a strong smell of eucalyptus, along with some other scents he couldn't identify coming from the diffuser. It was easing his ability to breathe. The cough syrup had given a moment of heat on his tongue before spreading warmth through his chest and, mercifully, quieting the endless tickle.

A deep exhaustion dragged on him. It clogged his ability to question the odd turn of events. One of the women had turned down the bed and the grey sheets were whispering to him. Spilling his clothes on the floor, Evan fell in.

The mist emanating from the diffuser slowly opened his sinuses and loosened the tightness in his chest. He dropped gratefully into sleep.

***

The women made their way back to Jan's cabin. When they reached the place where the path curved up behind the storefronts, Enoch edged past them, trotting to the electric box. He looked back questioningly, his hand poised above the switch.

"Go ahead," Becca called. The lights behind them extinguished.

"Are you sure?" Ophelia asked. "Our guest may wander and we don't want him ending up in the pond."

"I dosed him with your cough syrup, girl. He's out cold for the night," Felicity said.

Enoch was still waiting at the crest of the path, "Thank you for checking," Jan said. "He is indeed a very sick man. Did you have enough supper?"

The man nodded vigorously. "Yes, Miss Jan."

"Then, goodnight. We'll see you at breakfast."

"Breakfast," he repeated carefully. "Yes." He turned and climbed the short path to a small travel trailer parked beside Becca's cabin. The women listened to hear his door close before heading back to Jan's cabin.

Felicity rinsed and loaded the dishwasher with the dinner dishes while Jan sliced the blueberry pie. "Who wants whipped cream and who wants ice cream?" she called to Ophelia and Becca in the living room. They called back their preferences.

Jan carried two plates while Felicity followed with the other two. "Okay, just so you know, this is the last of the blueberries," she said as she handed off the plates before taking hers from Felicity. Cutting a bite, she loaded it on her fork and then stared at the utensil she let hover midway between the plate and her mouth. "So what's your take on our guest in the Crone, Ophelia?"

Setting her plate on the low round table, Ophelia swallowed what she was chewing. "He looks like a man who has unexpectedly fallen on hard times. The sports jacket he was wearing was expensive when it was bought. Same with his shoes. "

Becca nodded. "I found his wallet in the console. I think he is pretty close to dead broke. He only had twenty-three dollars in his wallet. No debit or credit cards."

Jan looked at her sharply. "Don't you think that is a bit rude—prying into the man's business?"

"Ummm, we just took in a man we know nothing about, so a soupçon of caution is not unreasonable," Becca answered. "But, maybe more to the point, did we just take in Ophelia's predicted bad moon, ill wind, or shit storm?"

"Interesting," Felicity said thoughtfully. "This man is ill and he just kinda blew into our parking lot."

"Okay, it looks like our ill wind has apparently arrived. Pretty easy fix. A little medicine, a little food, and he can blow himself out of town when he is ready and able. Don't even need a protection spell for this one," Jan said as she stood up to gather the dessert plates.

"Or we could keep him," Ophelia said, tilting her head thoughtfully.

<h1 style="text-align:center">Chapter Two</h1>

It was the fifth day since Evan had found shelter in the little cabin. He awakened feeling nearly normal. A feeling that stayed with him as he showered, dressed, and packed his duffle bags. In addition to receiving medication, food, and uninterrupted rest, the ladies had washed the clothes he had stuffed in a garbage bag. Although faintly embarrassed at the thought of strangers washing his socks and shorts, he was grateful he wouldn't have to spend any of his few remaining dollars at the laundromat.

There was a light knock on the door. Crossing to it, he realized he no longer struggled to breathe. A short, thickset man staring at his feet was waiting on the other side. He tilted his head toward Evan without actually raising it. "Miss Felicity... she say breakfast... she say come." The man's eyes darted around Evan's periphery as though searching for something. "Please," he finally added, nodding his head. "Yes, she say that, please." The man exhaled a relieved breath as he had apparently accomplished his mission.

Recognizing the man's efforts despite his deficiencies, Evan's reply was gentle. "Yes, I'll come. Thank you."

For the first time, the man dared to glance at him. Nodding, he took himself down the stairs and scurried toward the long building.

Evan pulled the door shut and followed. At the gravel path, he paused to draw in the cool, damp air. It was heavy with the scent of evergreens, moist soil, and the sweet smell of death transforming into humus. For a brief instance he remembered himself a boy among many scrambling up the Coast Range as they planted thousands of tiny tree seedlings in the bleak moonscape of the Tillamook Burn.

Looking around, he saw the man who had knocked at his door was stopped at the juncture of the path and the parking lot, staring worriedly back in his direction. Smiling and raising his hand, Evan strode after him.

Approaching the parking lot, Evan noted the board and batt building looked like something likely to have been in every western movie he had ever watched. There was a long stretch of stairs leading up to the wide wooden walkway running along the entire front. Four signs affixed to the overhang denoted it contained an outdoor store, herbal shop, some kind of gallery and a deli. The woman with the buzz cut he remembered was named Ophelia lifted her hand in greeting as she wheeled a small cart loaded with plants out the door of the herbal shop.

He raised his in answer before turning toward the deli. The man, waiting at the door, opened it for him. Felicity was behind the counter, flipping something in an electric fry pan. She smiled at Evan but spoke to the man who slipped in behind him.

"Enoch, would you please pour Mr. Hjort a cup of coffee?"

"Evan. Just call me Evan. I still look for my dad when anyone says Mr. Hjort."

She responded with a nod.

Looking around, he chose a small table for two near the back wall. He watched as the man called Enoch poured coffee into a heavy ceramic mug and then very carefully brought it to him.

The door opened and Becca leaned in. "Felicity, are you hogging my favorite helper?" Enoch lit up with a happy smile. "Come on, you. The worms have come in and I need them counted out." He immediately trotted to the door, disappearing along with Becca.

"And there goes my helper," Felicity sighed. She brought a plate with a croissant sandwich thick with eggs, bacon, and cheese and sided with a bowl of fruit to the table. Setting it in front of Evan, she pulled out the chair opposite him and sat down. "Becca's worms always win out over wiping tables and bringing dishes to the sink."

She noticed Evan just quietly watching. She gestured to the plate, "Please eat. It's much better hot."

"Only if you let me pay for it. I can't keep living on your largesse. All of you have already been amazingly generous."

She shrugged. "It's part of the rule we live by."

"Is this place like a religious order or something?"

"Not exactly, but we do serve." She didn't answer the question in his eyes. "Please, eat," she gestured again as the door opened and a heavy-set woman entered.

"Hey, Nancy," Felicity said as she got up to cross behind the counter. There was a moment of small talk as Felicity exchanged a white paper bag for the proffered cash. Then securing a cup of coffee, she returned to the table. She glanced at the untouched meal and then at Evan. He dutifully picked up the breakfast sandwich and bit into it. It was both hearty and delicious.

Felicity waited until he had made significant headway into the sandwich before speaking. "We are not ones to pry into other people's business; however, our observations seem to indicate you might be in the midst of a life change."

Evan sat back. A quick succession of emotions flashed across his face… pain, anger, hurt, and resignation. "Yeah, I guess that's one way to describe it."

"Would you have any need for some employment?"

"Do I look like that much of a charity case?" Evan asked softly.

"Not at all. And I certainly do not mean any offense. It's just that recently we put out a request for some much-needed help around here, and then you found our parking lot." She gave an enigmatic smile. "We are open to the concept that many things happen for a reason. We would be amiss if we failed to at least explore this coincidence."

"What kind of help are you looking for? All of you seem quite capable."

"And we are, but we are also getting older. Our stamina and energy don't seem to go as far as they used to."

"I can appreciate that," Evan said with a wry smile, touching the grey at his temples that threaded its way into his hair.

"In addition to running our businesses here, we also handle a lot of workshops and other," she hesitated for a moment, "events, particularly from spring through fall. Our businesses and the events we can handle, especially with the help of Enoch. It's the land that we can no longer stay on top of."

"Land?"

"Yes, this property. We called it Summerland… the locals call it Hag Hollow," she said without rancor, "It's twenty acres of natural wilderness. We keep our interference with nature to a minimum, but we also have to ensure that those who attend our various workshops, retreats, and events also keep care of the land within these boundaries and they themselves are not harmed."

"And this entails?"

"Keeping the paths clear of fallen branches, transplanting wild growth to a safer location, maintaining the gravel and bark-dusted paths, cleaning debris and garbage out of the pond, overseeing the wildlife to ensure they are not hurt or harassed, helping with the garden and Ophelia's herb beds, and perhaps, occasionally helping us keep people from wandering onto the property from the back area."

"Do you have a lot of problem with that?"

"Not too much. Usually just a random hiker or mushroom hunter. The locals tend to avoid us except to do business. They are rather stuck in that regard. Totem doesn't have a lot of choices."

Evan tilted his head in puzzlement. "Why would they avoid you?"

Felicity smiled. "They believe we are witches."

"Are you? Witches?"

"We are women who choose to walk a feminine spiritual path, but that doesn't fit well with the male-centric churches in town so they resort to tired tropes to stigmatize us in the eyes of the community."

"I'm male," Evan noted.

Felicity's smile broadened into a grin. "Yes. We noticed and we will not hold that against you unless you give us reason to."

Evan continued to stare at her. It may have been his imagination but it seemed something crackled for a moment in the air around her.

"We're offering free use of a cabin and meals plus two hundred dollars a week. We would like someone to stay through the whole of our busy season, but if that is not workable, we will gladly accept what time might be available."

The door opened and Enoch appeared holding a travel mug. He held it in Felicity's direction. "Miss Becca say…" He stopped and his mouth moved soundlessly as he searched for a word.

Evan noticed Felicity just sat silently watching, giving the man space to achieve his objective.

"Two. She say that… two."

"Okay, two shots it is," she said as she got up from the chair and headed to the espresso machine sitting against the back wall. Enoch reached across the counter to hand her the cup.

"There better not be worm on that handle," she said taking the cup.

The man shook his head. "No. No worm."

While Evan watched the woman prepare the espresso, he contemplated the offer. He hadn't actually done any physical outdoor work in years. They had had a landscaping service care for the yard. And he was on his way to— where was he heading? Oh yeah, nowhere. At this moment, he was between the burned-out hulk of the life he once had and the black hole of a future.

When Enoch was out the door, Felicity returned to the table, refreshing both of their cups with the carafe she brought.

Sitting back down, she picked up her cup and sipped. Evan knew she was expecting an answer. That, too, was something he had apparently lost—his former ability to immediately make quick decisions. Likely because a lot of those decisions had ended up biting his ass badly.

"Are you familiar with the term 'Summerland'?" she asked unexpectedly, looking at him.

He shook his head, "No."

"Some believe it to be a place of rest between lives here on earth. An interlude allowing for reflection, healing, and planning for the next life. That is why we named our property Summerland. It is our intent to provide a space for that same reflection, healing, and planning for the next phase of life. Death is not a requirement."

Her words sank into the deep pain within him. He looked out the window beside him. Across the parking lot, he saw the sun dusting the upper branches of the Douglas firs and the still shadowy path, along the pond's edge, listing down to the cabins. Her words stirred recognition within him. Without even realizing he was doing it, he whispered, "Yes."

He didn't take his eyes from the window. Felicity wasn't sure if he was talking to her or to himself. Yes, he thought. That is what I need. Space. Space to grieve, space to settle with the past, space to find a way into the future.

He now looked at the woman. "Yes. I would very much appreciate the opportunity."

A warm smile greeted his answer. "We'll give you a property tour after we close up for the day. Fortunately, there is plenty of light this time of the year. That will give you some time to unpack and settle. I hope the cabin will work for you. We do have two others you are welcome to choose from, but I warn you, they are decorated frillier than the Crone."

He shook his head. "Where I am is just fine."

"Okay, for meals, breakfast and lunch here. We take turns cooking dinner for all of us. Feel free to raid the snack racks here or in Becca's store anytime. She carries the healthy stuff, I carry the junk. Make sure you keep some in the cabin for between meals or midnight munchies. And now I need to prep for lunch." She gathered up his dishes and refilled his cup from the carafe. "You can bring it back at lunch." She smiled and made for the small kitchen.

Stepping outside the door, Evan stared across the parking lot. He had the oddest sensation that even as he was looking over the land, somehow it was looking him over as well.

Chapter Three

Deep in arid New Mexico, a man turned the key and pushed into the cut-rate motel room, the air still fetid with the smell of the previous occupants. He lowered his shoulder, letting the motorcycle saddlebags slide to the floor before setting the battered guitar case beside them. He crossed the room to sit down on the bed's too thin mattress. Looking around, he realized it was indistinguishable from hundreds of others. He wondered how many broken-down bedsprings and mattresses he had slept on through the years as he crisscrossed the country chasing something he once called freedom? How much booze? How many drugs? One-nighters? When had his life become just an endless cycle of bad habits and bad decisions? Janis Joplin had sung freedom was just another word for nothing left to lose. He guessed that was about right. He truly had nothing left to lose.

He tried to calculate how much longer until he made it back to the place he swore he would never return to. A week? Maybe more? He dodged the knowledge he might not make it at all.

He wondered what it was like after all these years. It had been a helleva long time since he rode out, pulling a wheelie in celebration as he rode away from his previous life. What had come and gone? Who had come and gone? As the faded memories drifted through his mind, he pushed back the one question that burned deeper than all the others. Had she stayed or gone?

Trey Rossiter took it as a good omen that, just as he rode in, a ray of sunshine broke through the overcast sky illuminating the green sign announcing he had reached the township limits of Totem. There still didn't seem much in the way of traffic on the highway running through the town. He eased off the throttle and cruised slowly along, looking for familiar landmarks. There was change, but not change.

He noted the raggedy old Calhoun hunting and fishing lodge had been both expanded and cleaned up. A sign at the far end of the building said Calhoun Outdoor Store. He knew the old man would be dead after all these years. He wondered which of the boys had taken over the business. He swung his bike off the road, stopping at the edge of the parking area and flipping up the visor on his helmet.

Beside it was a sign reading Swanner's Green Apothecary. Was that Ophelia Swanner? She had been a weird one and everyone knew her mother was just flat out strange. Scanning to the next one, he didn't recognize who the Dressler in Dressler's ARTifacts was. He guessed it was some kind of art store or something with the first three letters capitalized.

His eyes drifted to the last sign on the building. He started and inadvertently killed the engine when it identified that business as Felicitations Deli. Felicity? Ghosts from the past swarmed out of the gravel, engulfing him with an overwhelming urge to back up and ride out of town. Abruptly, the exhaustion he had been holding at bay rolled in, swamping him. He didn't have it in him. The road had claimed it all over the years. Like it or not, this was as far as he could go now.

Although partially hidden by the lay of the land, he saw someone close the door to one of the cabins. Squinting, he realized there were only three now. There had been what… six or seven stashed among the trees when old man Calhoun had the property? Truth was they were more like shacks with wood floors back then. Rumors had kicked around town that some of the wives supplemented their household budget in those cabins. Calhoun wasn't particular about what went on as long as he got paid up front. His only hard and fast rule had been don't burn 'em down.

He could now see a man crossing the parking lot towards the stairs. As he watched, he wondered if he should know the person. He shook his head. Time had faded so much of his memory to barely decipherable images.

Leaving his visor up, he kicked the motorcycle to life and crossed the few yards of gravel, stopping at the railroad tie serving as protection from running directly into the stairs. The man had disappeared inside one of the storefronts.

He shut off the engine and pushed down the kickstand before tugging the helmet off his head, running a practiced hand through his thick, overlong hair, the black long faded away to silver-white. His leathers squeaked as he swung his leg over the seat. Out of habit, he reached for his guitar and saddlebags. Before he could pull them off, his heart began to pound until it felt like it was trying to slam right out of his chest wall. He grabbed onto the handlebar of his motorcycle and pushed his fist into the seat as he willed himself to make it through the episode.

Ophelia stepped outside the door to her shop, watering can in hand. She glanced at the parking lot, taking in the man leaning on his motorcycle. She watched as he carefully straightened up. His shoulders rose and fell as he drew in a couple of breaths before reaching for his belongings, his hand hesitating, then withdrawing. Instead it was only his helmet he carried by the chinstrap as he made his way to the stairs.

Although he didn't look in her direction, Ophelia was struck by the thought she had known this man somewhere in her past. There was something so familiar in his lanky movement. Just as he opened the door to the deli and stepped in, she dropped the watering can.

"Oh, Mother God," she whispered.

***

He stopped just inside, staring at the back of the woman behind the counter slicing ribbons of lettuce from a head with firm, quick strokes. Her thick, wavy hair was nearly all steely grey and no longer reached her waist. Time had added girth to her waist and hips but it was definitely her.

"Hello, Felicity."

Her head snapped up and her back went rigid. She put both hands on the counter, her right still resting over the handle of the knife, as she steadied herself. She had not heard the deep rumble of that voice in over fifty years. She expected to never hear it again.

She reached for the cloth beside the cutting board, carefully wiping her hands before turning.

Her last image of Trey Rossiter was of a tall, virile man with black hair and moustache, a slow, easy smile, and a way of drifting insouciantly through the days they had shared. The man standing in front of her was a faded, creased version; the years deeply etched in his visage evidenced the hard living he had apparently done during his long absence.

It wasn't his appearance that surprised her as much as her own feelings as she stared at him. The anger, hurt, and loss that had overwhelmed her when he first disappeared were barely perceptible memories. The seething tides of emotional turmoil had ebbed away without her noticing in the intervening decades.

Evan sat in his usual place in the corner watching Felicity and the man. He surmised there was some kind of history between them in the looks they exchanged. His suspicions seemed to be confirmed when Becca and Ophelia's faces appeared in the window beside him as they peered in.

"I sure could use a cup of coffee, if you happen to have one handy," the man said, lifting his helmet in the direction of the stacked coffee mugs.

Felicity silently turned and pulled one down, setting it on the counter as she reached for the coffee pot. Evan noted the man's slow, guarded movements as he crossed to the counter and pulled out one of the stools. Setting his helmet on the counter, he unzipped his motorcycle jacket.

Placing the cup and a spoon in front of him, Felicity automatically pushed the bowls of sugar and creamer towards him. Turning away, she picked up the knife and resumed slicing the lettuce.

"You're still looking good, Felicity," he said as he watched her.

"We're divorced, Trey. Have been for over forty years."

He nodded. "Kinda figured. Guess it was 'bout the only thing you could do."

She turned back, her grey eyes darkly serious. "I waited five years. It took me that long to accept your sorry ass wasn't coming back."

He looked past her shoulder. "I just needed some space to work through… stuff. I told myself I was just gonna ride for a couple of weeks, get my head in a better place. But there was always another road calling my name. One day I just looked up and realized twenty years had passed. Didn't seem right to try to come back then."

"And now?"

He tapped his chest. "The ticker's gone bad." He looked down as he slowly turned his cup in a circle before looking back at her. "When you find yourself in a stare-down with the grim reaper, you realize you might oughta try to make some things right while you can."

"There's only one thing you can do that will make things right with me," Felicity said quietly. He dipped his chin, staring silently into his coffee.

A cell phone began to ring. She scooped it up, then moved to a small pad lying next to the cash register and swiftly jotted down information. "Give me twenty, Pam, before you pick up."

Disconnecting, she slipped the phone into her apron pocket as she turned to the counter and began to deal out slices of bread. She felt curiously detached as if she had just interacted with a ghost she had long ago given up noticing. The only thing she would ever want from Trey Rossiter now was the truth about the night he walked in soaked in her brother's blood.

Chapter Four

Mona Weiner was carefully pushing her polishing cloth into the grooves of the scrollwork of the pulpit when the church pastor leaned around the door leading from the hall.

"Mona?" He looked perplexed as he scanned the seemingly empty sanctuary.

Pushing herself to her feet, her ungainly form emerged from behind the pulpit. She gripped her cleaning cloth tightly, her breath catching for a moment as it always did when she first saw him.

"Oh, good, there you are," he said. "Pam's not back yet from taking her mother to the doctor so I need you to run over to the deli and pick up the sandwiches for the deacon's meeting. Come on back to the office and I'll get you a check."

The middle-aged woman quickly dropped the cloth in her cleaning tote and took a moment to smooth her smock before following. She arrived just as he was pulling the checkbook out of the church secretary's drawer. He flipped it open and ripped out the check. "Make sure you get a receipt for the records," he said as he signed it, shoving it in her direction before putting his pen to filling out the stub.

Picking up the check, Mona stared at it, a troubled look settling on her face. "Pastor, can I ask you something?"

"Sure."

"Are we committing a sin by getting lunch from the deli? Miss Kepler told me that those women are actually witches."

She was surprised at the distaste in his expression when he looked up at her. "Witches might not be exactly the right word, Mona, but it's close." Although his tone remained even, there was an underlying sharpness.

Mona's large, bland face became a question mark.

"You're relatively new to Totem so you wouldn't know, but those women have been a thorn in this town's side for a very long time. They have a penchant for getting into other people's business and it caused some real hardship for some of the folk here in Totem."

"So they aren't really witches?"

"No. Just a bunch of old biddies who never learned to accept their place in God's order," he answered with some heat. Noting Mona's eyes widen, Caleb forced a smile on his face. "The Bible is very clear on the role of females. When women fail to obey those tenets then they are living in opposition to the Word, which is why they get branded as witches. Better get those sandwiches because hungry deacons aren't going to be in the mood to start planning this year's revival."

He busied himself returning the checkbook to the drawer in which Pam kept the church financial records. A smattering of memories flitted unpleasantly through his thoughts. Those damned old women were destined to be his cross to bear until they went to their reward – in hell.

Mona considered the pastor's words as she drove the short distance to the deli. She wished old Miss Kepler hadn't said anything about witches. It was unsettling to feel she might be inadvertently exposing herself to evil, even with the words of Pastor Barnwell and Pam that they weren't what Miss Kepler said.

She breathed easier when she entered the deli and found church deacon Alan Newton already waiting at the counter. She was a bit taken aback to see him chatting with some old man dressed in a worn, dusty motorcycle outfit.

Felicity came out of the little kitchen and slipped a container into the white bag sitting on the counter. She added several packages of crackers before folding the top over and holding it in the deacon's direction. "Here you go, Alan."

He took the proffered bag with one hand while holding a twenty-dollar bill out with his other hand. "Keep the change, Felicity, for…" he hesitated a moment. "For Enoch's college fund."

Felicity gave him a knowing smile. "Tell Bethany hi," she said as she took the bill. Although it had been a very long time now, Alan was still paying it forward.

Behind him, Mona's brows drew together in puzzlement. Everybody knew that Enoch was retar… No, that wasn't right anymore. It was something else she couldn't remember. How come Deacon Newton was giving Felicity money for his college?

Swinging back to the man, the deacon held out his hand. "Good to see you, Trey. Let's find a time to sit down with a pot of Felicity's coffee and really catch up."

The man met the deacon's hand with his grease-stained one. "I'll look forward to it. You take care."

Turning toward the door, Deacon Newton almost ran into Mona. "Oh, hey, you going to be heading back to the church, Mona?"

She nodded, going tongue-tied as she always did in the presence of one of the church elders.

"Tell Caleb I'll be there for the meeting as soon as I drop this off at the office for Bethany," he said as he maneuvered around her and headed to the door, not waiting for her to nod again.

Mona moved up to the counter. She felt the eyes of the man Deacon Newton had been talking to staring at her. She took an uncomfortable side-step, turning her back to him.

Felicity picked up her order pad. "Hi, Mona. What would you like?

Mona shook her head. "I'm here to pick up the order for the church," she said pulling the check out of her purse.

Felicity picked up a box from the back counter. There was a receipt stapled to the top of one of the bags. Mona peered at it and then carefully wrote the amount on the check. As she handed it over, Felicity pointed to the receipt. "Make sure that Pam gets that for her records."

***

Pastor Barnwell was making his way around a table in the fellowship hall, setting packets in front of each of six chairs when Mona arrived bearing the box of white bags.

"Great timing, Mona. Just set it in the middle of the table. The men can sort out whose sandwich is whose. I think the coffee is done. Would you mind filling the carafe and grabbing some of the cups from the kitchen?"

"I saw Deacon Newton at the deli. He said to tell you that he would be here as soon as he dropped off lunch to Mrs. Newton," she said before dutifully trotting to the kitchen.

She was just placing the carafe and cups next to the food box when Alan Newton came in.

"Man, Caleb, you won't believe who I just saw at Felicity's," he said making for the table to rummage through the bags. "Trey Rossiter! I would have figured him long dead since no one has heard hide nor hair from him in, what's it been, must be fifty years?" He pulled a bag out.

Mona was startled to see the pastor blanch and his knuckles go white where he gripped the back of his chair. Even his voice had a different timbre when he responded. "You're kidding me. He just passing through?"

Unwrapping his sandwich, Alan peeked under the bread to assure himself it was to his liking. "Nope. Seems he's got some health problems now so he's come home to stay. I gotta say it looks like the years haven't been particularly good. Maybe you should look him up just in case he's ready to give up his sinning ways."

Pastor's reply was lost as the other deacons began to drift in and rustle through the bags. He noticed Mona waiting quietly to the side. He gave her one of his smiles that always liquefied her mid-section. "Thanks for all your help, Mona. I appreciate your willingness to jump in whenever I need you."

Although it was a dismissal, Mona wrapped her arms around her mid-section to hold onto the warmth it elicited within her.

Following the blessing of the food, the deacons ate and talked about the annual revival meeting. Even while discussing tent rentals, advertising and a budget, a question kept darting through Caleb's mind. How much grief was coming in the wake of Trey's return?

***

Trey pushed back the plate containing the remains of the lunch Felicity had set in front of him. "Your mama sure taught you well, girl. You can still make an egg sandwich sing."

As Felicity reached to take the plate, Trey leaned back and closed his eyes. His weathered face had a grayish tinge.

"Trey?"

He opened his eyes and gave the slow smile that at one time would have set her on fire. "I'm really bushed. I should go see if I can get a cabin from… I'm guessing the old man is dead. Which Calhoun boy took over the store?"

"None," Felicity answered. "Becca's got the store and the cabins aren't for rent."

"Then I guess I'll mosey on up to the Bed Well, see what Tom's got."

Felicity shook her head. "Trey, you're remembering a Totem that's long gone. The Bed Well was torn about twenty-five years ago and Tom has been dead at least a decade. If you're looking for a place to stay, you're going to have head back to the valley."

Shadows moved in his eyes as he looked at her. "I don't know I got it left in me, girl," he said softly.

Felicity stared at him. The last vestiges of the man she had once known in her youth disappeared. Sitting in front of her was an old, sick man. A man in need. For a moment, she felt a surge of hostility at the rules on which they had built Summerland. She blew out a conflicted breath.

"Enoch?"

The man came out of the kitchen wearing his waterproof apron and gloves.

"I need to run down to Becca's. Would you keep watch and let me know if anyone comes in before I'm back?"

He nodded his head, his expression a combination of guilelessness and pride. "Yes, Miss Felicity. I do that."

Felicity turned the key that locked the cash register and pulled it out.

Trey watched. "Looks like you don't trust me, Felicity."

"Some things haven't changed."

Chapter Five

Ophelia caught sight of Felicity striding past her shop. She skinned off her potting gloves and left the witch hazel cuttings lying.

Following her into the outdoor store, she heard Becca ask, "What the hell is Trey Rossiter doing back in Totem?" Ophelia circled Felicity to join Becca.

Felicity's expression was a mixture of frustration and irritation. "According to him, he came home to, and I quote, 'make some things right' before he dies."

Becca and Ophelia shot looks at each other. "Die?"

"Trey says his heart is failing. And," Felicity's voice dropped, "I don't think he's pulling a con this time. He looks pretty frail."

Becca crossed her arms over her chest. "Okay. So what's he expecting? You to welcome him like five decades haven't passed and provide him comfort in his final days?"

"I don't know what he expects. Honestly, it's almost like he has no real concept of how very long he has been away and that Totem is nothing like the town he rode out of. So much of what he's remembering is dead and gone."

"So where is he planning on staying?" Ophelia asked. "His sister sold off their folks' place years ago."

"I guess he knows that since he mentioned the cabins here, and when I told him they weren't for rent, he brought up the old Bed Well."

"Geez, that was torn down decades ago," Ophelia said.

"I told him that, too, and that there really wasn't any place in town anymore so he would have to head back to the valley." She paused. "He said that he didn't think he could make it."

"Sympathy ploy?" Becca asked.

Felicity stared past Becca's shoulder at the corkboard on the back wall covered in hunting and fishing regulation posters. Finally she shook her head. "No. His aura is telling me he is desperately ill."

The three women stood silent for a moment. Then Becca reached for her carabiner. "So what do you think he would prefer…pink or red?"

Felicity's eyes were troubled. "Do you really think that is the right thing to do?"

"Who knows?" said Ophelia. "But our rule says we don't let anyone die in a ditch if we can help it, so yeah, pink or red."

Felicity looked vexed as she reached for the keys. "Just remember, Trey Rossiter has always been trouble. He may be slowed down but I doubt his ways have changed much."

Becca and Ophelia watched her push back out the screen door. "I'm thinking our bad moon just rose," Ophelia said.

Becca nodded her agreement. "Time to get the amulets out."

***

Stalking back toward the deli, Felicity saw Trey was now sitting on the steps, supporting himself against one of the uprights, his eyes closed.

She slowed and then stopped. Suddenly, he wasn't the man who completely trashed her life at one time. He was, like her, just another of their generation gathering on life's exit platform, waiting their turn to be called off the planet.

She left him undisturbed as she ducked into the deli to check on Enoch. He was carefully wiping down each table and pushing the chairs in. "You good?" she asked.

He had on his solemn, responsible expression as he nodded.

"I'll be just a few more minutes."

Stepping back to where the man was sitting, she reached out and nudged his shoulder. "Trey?"

He started as if he had actually fallen asleep. He looked at her foggily.

"Come on, we have a place for you to stay if you want. You just have to decide whether your favorite color is pink or red." She started down the stairs.

Using the upright, he pushed himself to his feet and followed her across the parking lot to the path running along the front of the cabins. "I thought you said these weren't for rent."

Stopping at the first cabin, Felicity unlocked the door. "They aren't. We use them as shelter for people in need," she replied swinging the door open.

Although all three cabins were identical in layout, this one was decorated in shades of pink with frothy touches enhancing its feminine decor. The pictures on the wall exuded a virginal innocence.

Trey looked around. "It's awfully girly, isn't it?"

"That's why we call it the Maiden. Let's look at the other one and then you can make up your mind."

The next cabin was, as Felicity had said, red from bed coverings to pillows on the couch, although overall, the lines were sleeker and had a more mature feel than the previous one. The framed pictures on the wall were abstract with large swathes of red running through them.

"Don't know if I like the pictures much," Trey said looking around.

You'd like them a lot less if you knew they represented the fertility of menstruation and motherhood, Felicity thought. "This is all we have. The other cabin is already occupied by the man who helps keep our grounds up. So do you want one or not?"

***

Evan ambled along the trail running across the small ridge behind the cabins. Although he had only been working at Summerland for a few weeks, he was startled to find himself behaving in ways that were the antithesis of his former self who measured everything in productivity and money. That version would have been striding swiftly toward his objective of meeting Ophelia to work in the garden area. Today, he paused to listen to the tapping of a downy wood- pecker, then four harsh caws of a crow that were answered by two caws some- where deeper in the woods. Something flicked off a fallen log a few feet away. Squirrel? Chipmunk? He caught only the motion out of the corner of his eye.

He passed his hand over the rough bark of an old Douglas fir as he stepped around it. When Becca first showed him around the property, she pointed out an old-growth fir that had a small flat stone at its base.

"This is Grandfather Tree," she said. "We think he is the oldest tree in our forest. He is certainly the wisest. Got a problem, got a question, all you need to do is sit on the stone and lean against him. Tell him straight up what's going on. He's a slow talker but if you just sit and wait, he will answer."

Evan hadn't resorted to Grandfather Tree's wisdom yet. He was treading an emotionally neutral place that was neither past nor future. He wasn't sure what kind of answer a tree could possibly give, but he knew he wasn't ready to deal with the emotions that would be attached to any question he might ask of it—or himself.

He crested the top of the gravel pathway running down to the parking area. The garden cart sitting by the stairs was already loaded with starter trays and pots. Ophelia's gardening bucket was on the walkway just outside her store's entrance. After angling his way to the parking lot, Evan climbed the steps and leaned in the Green Apothecary's doorway.

"Ready for me to pull the wagon up?"

"Yup. I'll be right behind you after I let Jan know so she can keep an eye on the shop for me. Don't park the cart in the sun. There are babies on board."

Evan nodded at her admonition as he headed back down the stairs and grabbed the handle. As he pulled it over the gravel toward the garden area, he took care not to jostle Ophelia's 'babies' too much. When he realized what he was doing, he shook his head at himself. They were just plants, after all. He started to pick up his pace, but the gravel abruptly began to bind the turn of the wheels on the cart, refusing to let him go faster than the original pace he had set. He stopped to look at the cart. He had used it several times to take buckets of compost from the pile behind the storefronts up the rise to the gardens and was never slowed down even by the weight.

Evan turned and tried to step up his pace again. Again, the wheel bound up. Sighing, he recognized this was, apparently, another of what he mentally labeled the inexplicables that kept cropping up around him. He didn't understand them but he had come recognize they were relentless in what they expected from him. He set off slowly pulling the plants up to the garden beds.

He had just positioned the cart in the dapple light provided by the gently moving fir branches when Ophelia appeared with her bucket of hand tools and plant potions.

Setting the bucket down beside the cart, she pointed to six trays of tiny seedlings. "So these need to go in the tunnel to harden off before we tuck them into their beds." She grabbed a tray and headed in the direction of the hoop house at the far edge of the garden beds. Evan picked up a tray in each hand and followed. He set them on the low earth-covered table inside the tunnel and headed back for the remaining trays. Ophelia was busy shuffling pots around to position each tray under one of the openings in the side of the green plastic mesh covering the metal framing arches.

"Evan, would you unzip and tie up the opening covers, please," she asked. "Just on this side today."

Outside the tunnel, he unzipped the four window coverings, rolling up the plastic and tying them so unobstructed fresh air and light flowed inside the protective shelter.

Ophelia came out, wiping her hands on the edge of her denim apron. "We'll need to close up the windows in a couple of hours. Tomorrow we'll open them up an hour earlier and close them an hour later. It will take about ten days before those seedlings will be ready to face the wide open spaces without it killing them."

She moved back to the cart and began categorizing the remaining pots. "These go in the herb bed, these in the veggie patch, and these in the medicinal beds. Wanna grab those cucumbers," she said pointing to the pots identified as veggies, "while I get the trowels?"

Dropping the trowels at the edge of the garden, Ophelia began to take the pots from Evan, spacing them along the worked ground.

"Did you notice you're getting a neighbor?" Ophelia asked when they were on their knees carefully tipping the plants out the pots, gently spreading their roots, and settling them into the bed.

Evan paused in tucking the soil around the one he was planting. "Neighbor? Someone else moving into one of the cabins?"

Ophelia sat back on her haunches and wiped her forehead. "Should have brought my hat. It's warmer than I thought. Yeah. You might have seen him at lunch today."

"The motorcycle guy?" Evan guessed. Although he didn't know names, he had begun to recognize the regular customers at Felicitations by sight.

"Yeah, Trey Rossiter," she said with some antipathy. "A bit of ancient Totem history come back to haunt us all, especially Felicity."

"I thought I saw some connection between them when he came in."

"That man damn near destroyed her. Mom tried to warn her. She said it was like he was a black storm that was going to wreak a whole lot of trouble. But Felicity was young—hell, we all were—and stupid in love. She couldn't see anything except Trey. In the end, Mom was right."

"So you and Felicity grew up here?"

"Me, Felicity, and Becca, along with Trey. He was best buds with Felicity's older brother, Duane. They were peas in a pod. Wild-ass, hellraising stoners who loved nothing more than to rip up the town every chance they got."

"Her brother still in Totem?"

"Yes," Ophelia reached for another pot. "And no."

Evan paused to look his question at her.

An odd brew of sadness and bitterness passed over Ophelia's face. "He's in the graveyard and Trey Rossiter may have helped put him there."

Chapter Six

Dawna Barnwell pushed into the kitchen from the garage. As soon as she reached the island, she let loose the multiple items she held in her arms. "Caleb, I'm home," she called. "I picked up Chinese for supper."

Her husband made his way to the kitchen, pausing to lean against the door jamb as he watched his wife deftly sort and put away the tumbled notepads and books she had carried in. In a few moments, the only thing remaining was the large white bag containing dinner.

Dawna was now pulling plates out of the cupboard, followed by silverware from the drawer. After setting two places, she began emptying the bag of various sized boxes. "Remind me to strangle Miss Kepler after services next Sunday. I got you kung pao chicken. They were out of spring rolls so we have pot stickers instead."

Sliding onto one of the counter stools, Caleb waited for his wife to finish arranging the food and seat herself before saying the blessing over the food.

"Dear ancient Miss Kepler? What horrendous thing has she been up to now?" Caleb asked, filling his plate from the various containers.

"Apparently, she made some comment about the Hag Hallow women being witches and now Mona is seeing black cats and cauldrons under every rock. She is convincing herself that they are leaving invisible trails of evil that will ensnare her, threatening her future sainthood."

"We don't do saints," Caleb said forking up some of the fiery chicken.

"You know what I mean. Since her aunt died, the church has become her life. She wants so desperately to be worthy," Dawna reached for the pot stickers, "of your attention."

Caleb pulled a face. He was more than aware of Mona's hero worship. Actually, pretty much everyone in the church was aware of it. It had become something of a joke among the congregation.

Silence settled as they ate. Finally, setting her fork down and leaning back, Dawna broke it. "So, I talked with Pam at the meeting. She's probably going to have to be taking more time off to deal with her mother's health issues."

"That's going be a problem since we're gearing up for the annual revival. My time needs to be directed to writing my sermons, figuring out the music, the promotion and advertising. I don't have time to deal with the…"

"Scut work?" Dawna said, beginning to close the tops on the cartons holding leftovers.

Caleb didn't argue with her choice of words as he pushed his plate forcefully away. "Exactly." He blew out an exasperated breath. "I just don't need any more bad news right now."

She raised an eyebrow.

"You didn't hear? Trey Rossiter has come back to Totem."

She lifted a shoulder. "Who's Trey Rossiter?"

"You remember. He was…" Caleb paused. No, Dawna wouldn't remember. They had been married so long he sometimes forgot that she wasn't originally from Totem. "Trey Rossiter is someone who grew up and went to school the same time as me. He disappeared out of town about the time I headed off to Bible college. No one's seen or heard from him in decades. Now Alan tells me he's back in town…saw him at the deli."

Dawna shrugged again. "So?"

"Trust me, where Trey Rossiter walks, the devil is not far behind."

Letting her husband's hyperbole about some long-ago schoolmate blow past her, Dawna stored the leftovers in the refrigerator before putting the dishes in the dishwasher and wiping the kitchen island. "So, did you talk with the deacons about doing the workshop for the women during the men's consecration program?"

Caleb gave his wife a not-quite-patient look. "I held off because I realized that we always follow up the consecration service with refreshments before we start the evening service. I figured your hands would be too full overseeing the setting up of the food and cleanup to try to add something else to the mix."

As the subject was already closed in his mind, he gave no weight to the crack of lightning that flashed in her eyes. Placation was delivered by abstractedly patting her hand still holding the dishcloth. "I'm sorry, hon, but you will still be doing the Lord's work. That's the important part after all." He gave one more pat before disengaging by standing up. "I gotta work on my sermon for Sunday. Thanks for dinner."

She stared at his retreating back in stunned disbelief. He had cavalierly tossed aside something she had been developing and planning for the past year to, once again, relegate her to the menial and irrelevant. A thought popped un-bidden into her head. *No, it isn't the Lord you want me to serve—it's you.* The resentment that had begun to curdle the beliefs she had once held so tight-ly notched up. She balled up the cloth, slam-dunking it into the sink before stalking to her own office space carved out of her bedroom. She fought the overriding urge to slam the door in the face of her husband's utter callousness.

Slumping against it, she stared at the neat stack of folders on her desk holding her yearlong research into the place and purpose of women in the 21st century church and particularly their church. Except it wasn't their church. It was his church.

The bubble of anger collapsed. Dispirited, she moved to huddle into the small recliner; staring numbly at the cross on the wall opposite her as she ran her memory over past revivals. When the church doors opened following the consecration service, the men streamed immediately to the food tables, filling their plates with the sandwiches, salads, and desserts the women had spent the day preparing. Intent on their empty bellies, they seldom even seemed to see the women who dashed back and forth from the fellowship hall to the kitchen replenishing the rapidly emptying bowls and platters. When sated, they drifted back to the tent that acted as the sanctuary or outside to visit until it was time for the evening service, leaving the women with the cleanup.

For the women, it was a foot race to get everything cleaned up and left-over food stored in order to make the service. Caleb didn't like his evening production interrupted so the women were exiled to the tent they set up for the overflow crowds.

Dawna tilted her head. Production? What an odd descriptor to apply to the revival services. Then she realized that, while it was an odd word, it was also the perfect word. Caleb loved wrapping his revival sermons in spotlights, dramatic music, and, if possible, special effects. Cameras caught his every move, every expression, and word, broadcasting them to a big-screen TV in the main and side tent. Twenty-first century preaching.

A chafing under her skin was growing into unbearableness. Leaning back, she closed her eyes as a sense of becoming unmoored pulled her farther in a growing unhappiness. The faith that had carried her for so many decades was beginning to crack. Seeping through was a small, but insistent, hunger that she couldn't even name. A hunger that was beginning to pound to the rhythm of rebellion.

Chapter Seven

As there were now seven mouths to feed at dinnertime, it had been decided everyone would eat dinner in the deli, except Enoch, who preferred to eat in his little camp trailer while watching his beloved children's shows.

After offering to help, and being flagged off by the women, Evan collected a glass of iced tea and made his way to the little table in the back where he usually sat. Staring out the window, he saw Trey making his way toward the building. Although the incline up from the cabins was gentle, he saw the man stop several times to seemingly catch his breath. When he finally came through the door, Evan noted the cool glances three of the women gave him while Felicity didn't bother to turn. Ophelia pushed one of the iced tea glasses lined up on the counter in his direction.

Picking it up, Trey took a sip before looking around the room. Spotting Evan in the back, he made his way in his direction. "Mind?" he asked, his hand already on the chair back. Evan motioned for him to sit.

Setting his glass on the table, he held out his hand. "Trey Rossiter."

Evan took it. "Evan Hjort."

Trey folded himself into the chair.

"How long have you been in Totem?" Trey asked.

"Only a few weeks."

"How did you get hooked up with the girls?"

Evan shrugged. "Happenstance, I guess."

The brief conversation ended when Jan arrived with a crab louie salad in each hand, setting them in front of the men. She returned a moment later with a bowl of dressing and a plate of garlic toast. Trey looked at her quizzically. "Do I know you?" he asked.

"Nope," she said succinctly before heading to the larger table at the other end of the room where the women were gathering.

Glancing at Trey's plate and then his own, Evan noted the difference. "You didn't get any asparagus," he said.

"Don't like it. Felicity knows that." Trey stared at his plate for a very long moment. "Damn, she was the best thing that ever happened to me," he said softly before looking up at Evan. "Ever realize you made some really bad decisions in life?"

Evan stabbed a chunk of crab. "Every single day."

Looking over Trey's shoulder as he ate, Evan noted the women seemed to be engaged in a working dinner as notepads, phones, and tablets intermingled with their food and drink.

***

"So has Caleb posted what weekend Brother Love's Traveling Salvation Show is going to happen this year?" Becca asked.

Jan wiped her fingers on a napkin before scrolling through her tablet. "Ummm, it looks like it is going to be August 17th, 18th, and 19th," she said.

"Do we want our retreat the weekend before or the weekend after?" Becca asked.

"How about we do it the weekend of and really torque him?" Ophelia suggested.

"Lovely thought, but you know what a nightmare parking is around here. Don't need our ladies having to hike miles down the highway," Becca noted.

"Let's do it the weekend after. A kinda interim before so many get caught up in the 'back to school' drill. Plus Caleb always takes that week off so there shouldn't be anyone standing around in our parking lot trying to proselytize our attendees." Jan suggested.

"Gee, I would miss Dawna and her group with their little set-up on the edge of the parking lot trying to save the souls of all the wicked heathens who come," Felicity said.

Ophelia reached for a piece of garlic toast. "Speaking of Dawna, I saw her today at Seb's when I was picking up the lemons and lettuce. She was definitely not radiating her usual 'happy, happy, look at me, my life is perfect' self. In fact, she actually spoke to me."

Jan looked floored. "You're kidding. She usually goes around me like I'm carrying cooties or something."

"It's the dreads and tats," Becca said. "Old ladies should be wearing prim little bobs, not long bead-accented dreadlocks and full-sleeve tattoos."

"And all those wild boho dresses with your cutaway jean jacket, girl. Really what are you thinking?" Felicity teased.

"Yeah, did the prim bob with the proper heels for decades and they ate massive holes in my soul. I got judged by suburbia's best. Believe me, Dawna Barnwell and her pursed-lipped buddies couldn't hold a candle to them."

Felicity nodded. "Yup, if the opinion of others was of any consequence, Summerland wouldn't exist. So back to the business at hand. Do we agree that we should do the weekend before Labor Day for our annual 'freak the local churches out' event?"

***

Trey leaned back in his chair with a satisfied sigh. "About the only way that would be more perfect would be by finishing it off with an ice-cold beer. Care to join me?" he asked Evan.

Standing up, Evan gathered the dishes. "Sounds great. Let me take these back to the kitchen and I'll be right along."

He paused at the counter and looked over at the women.

"Just leave them there and we'll take care of them. Thanks, Evan," Felicity said.

Trey's pace was so slow he had just reached his cabin when Evan strode up behind him. Pulling himself up the stairs, he dropped on the bench beside the door. "Beer's in the refrig," he said. "Door's not locked."

Evan shot a concerned look at the man before entering the cabin and getting two beers out. He untwisted the tops before stepping back outside and handing one off to Trey.

Trey took a pull off the bottle. "Getting old sure does suck, Hjort."

Settling himself on the top step, Evan took a sip of his own beer before nodding in agreement. "Sure does, and it's a hell of a time to try and decide what you want to do when you grow up."

"Sounds like life took a dog leg on you."

"More like ran me off a cliff I should have seen coming." This was a conversation path Evan realized he didn't want to go down with a near stranger. He abruptly changed the subject. "Ophelia tells me you and some of the women all grew up together here."

Trey nodded. "Yup, right here is the middle of nowhere. Town was so small back then that if you sneezed coming into it, you would have missed it." He stared out at the highway. "Even so, me and Duane had some times here."

"Friend or family?"

"Both, I guess. Duane was Felicity's older brother. He was my friend growing up and when I married Felicity, we were family."

"You were married to Felicity?"

"Once upon a time, yeah. She was this skinny little kid that was always hanging around bugging Duane and me. Tattled on us all the time. A real pain in the ass. Then one day, I turned around and she was this gorgeous woman. Damn, I found myself wanting to hang with her instead of Duane. Eventually, it seemed like the only smart thing to do was to marry her. It was the best time of my life," he finished softly.

Evan sipped his beer as the man floated in his memories.

Trey pulled in a deep breath. "Might have stayed that way if Duane hadn't died. Yeah, that changed everything." Trey leaned back against the cabin wall staring into his past. "Me and Duane loved to ride the back roads. The wind blowing in our faces… helmets weren't required yet. It was like we were Peter Fonda and Dennis Hopper in Easy Rider. We were riding one evening, just at twilight. Pickup came ripping out of a side road, fishtailing in the gravel and sideswiped Duane. Crushed his leg and severed his femoral artery. I got him off the road and was fixing to head back for help—weren't any cell phones then—when a car came by and went for me. I tried to stop the bleeding with my belt while waiting for the ambulance to come from town."

A deep silence settled before he continued in a voice Evan could barely hear. "He was gone by the time they got there."

A slight breeze brushed by Evan and an odd feeling settled between his shoulder blades. It felt like someone had passed him on their way up to the porch.

"Thing of it was, I always had a feeling that it wasn't just a bad bit of luck. When the shock kinda wore off, I felt like maybe that pickup had been waiting for us. I remembered the sound of an engine revving just before it happened."

"Did they ever catch the person?"

Trey took another swallow of his beer. "Nope. Didn't have enough to go on. A little paint was about it and it was rattle-can paint to boot. Totem was a poor town back then. Most every truck in town had rattle-can paint on it."

"You didn't recognize it? You said Totem was pretty small; would have guessed you might know who owned most of the rigs."

"Happened too fast. Didn't really get a good look. Might not even have been from Totem. It was summer. Lots of people from the Valley head to the back country then."

Listening to the silence once again stretching between them, Evan got a feeling in his gut Trey did know who killed his brother-in-law. But that made no sense. Why would he pretend he didn't?

Evan shivered slightly for a moment as the air suddenly chilled. The sensation passed quickly and Evan wondered if he had just imagined it given their macabre topic.

"I was surprised to see that Becca ended up with the outdoor business. Thought one of the boys would have." Evan mentally scrambled for a moment to catch up to Trey's abrupt change in the conversation.

"Boys?"

"Yeah, Becca had two older brothers. 'Course they might have beat feet out of here as soon as they were able. Old man Calhoun was a real hard-assed bastard. Worked those kids unmercifully, especially after the wife died. Heard tell he was pretty free with his belt and fists as well. Most of the town steered clear of him other than doing what business they had to with the store. About the only person who wasn't afraid was Ophelia's mother."

Trey suddenly grinned. "She caught him slapping poor Becca around one day. Stopped him cold and threatened to curse him into an early grave if he ever raised another hand to the kids. After that, she'd stop in the store once in a while just to stare at him. Made him as nervous as a cat in a roomful of rocking chairs. Yeah, Eleanora was one crazy lady."

"Not sure I understand why that would deter him?"

"Eleanora was a witch, or at least most of Totem sure believed she was. People always gave her a wide berth, although I'd bet my bike most every one of them snuck up to her door at one time or another looking for a bit of what she was selling."

"Such as?"

"Eleanora cast horoscopes, read the tarot cards, and had a way with plants that even the best gardeners in town couldn't duplicate. She had a houseful of little jars and bottles she claimed could cure most anything that ailed you. The thing that really got to people was her habit of walking up to them out of the blue and telling them things."

"What kind of things?" Evan asked curiously.

"Don't really know for sure. She always kept it private between herself and whoever, but I guess she got it right more often than not because it made people real nervous when they saw her coming for them, although some seemed real grateful later.

"I liked her although she and I got into it a couple of times because she kept trying to warn Felicity off from marrying me. Said I would just break her heart. I swore I wouldn't." Trey looked down at the beer bottle he was turning in his hands. "But I did."

Silence again stretched in the twilight.

"Anyway, makes me wonder if Ophelia followed in her witchy mama's footsteps."

Evan swallowed the last of his beer. "Don't really know except she does seem to apparently have her way with plants from what you said. And speaking of plants, I better head off. Ophelia's doing some kind of herbal workshop tomorrow and I gotta be up at the crack of dawn to help get her stuff down here. Thanks for the beer, Trey."

"Yeah, I was told to keep myself scarce. Maybe I'll take a little ride around and see what's changed. Nice talking with you, Hjort. Feel free to stop by anytime you need a cold brew. Always got some in the fridge." Evan caught a sense of a deep loneliness intertwined in the man's words.

"I'll do that," he replied before heading down the path to his cabin.

Shutting down things down for the night, Evan pondered on the fact that he had now heard the word 'witches' referenced twice in connection with the women. Not that it bothered him, but how do you even identify if someone is a witch and what exactly do witches do? He realized that pretty much his entire knowledge consisted of Wendy the Good Little Witch in the Casper the Friendly Ghost comic books he inherited from his older sister and what he remembered from the required reading of The Crucible in some class or another he took in college. It didn't really matter. He was just planning on staying for the season the women needed him to build a nest egg before he headed off to the future he still didn't have a clue about.

Chapter Eight

Across the small town, witches were circling in someone else's thoughts. Mona stacked the fried chicken and potato salad she had picked up at Seb's grocery store deli on a paper plate. Seb's potato salad was nowhere near as good as what she could get at Felicitations, but she was now afraid she would be giving her money to support whatever wickedness might be happening there.

She turned on the radio by the recliner in the small, cluttered living room. It was always tuned to a Christian broadcast station. She rarely turned on the TV across from her. Much of what was being broadcast today seemed to be nothing but sex and violence. The few times she tried to watch one program or another she had heard people talk about at church, she always felt like a dirty film was settling on her so she stuck to her radio.

When the chicken was just bones, she washed the grease off her hands after tossing the remains in the overflowing trash can in her kitchen. Her aunt would have never allowed the house to have become as cluttered and messy as it was now. And for a long time after her aunt passed, leaving the house to Mona, it had been maintained to those standards. But as she had centered her life more and more around the church and its programs, the rest of her life had descended into entropy.

Back in her chair, she reached for her Bible and the printed pages resting under it. It was a programmed reading list Pam had handed out in one of their Bible study groups. Each day listed a selection from the Old Testament, the New Testament, and Psalms. Meticulously sticking to the daily readings, she would have read the whole Bible by the end of the year.

She struggled with the daily reading. She was a slow reader who frequently was stymied with what the words were conveying, but she faithfully dug in each evening.

When she had dutifully worked her way through each section, she sat straining after the knowledge Pastor Barnwell said every Sunday was there. No illumination or fire of faith engulfed her. With a sigh, she sat the Book aside and reached for the bag on the floor beside her chair.

She pulled out the lap robe she was currently crocheting for the church women's circle. It was a simple stitch that let her mind drift between the words she had just read, the music on the radio, and her moving hands.

As her hook slid through the stitches and grabbed the yarn, she thought about the beautiful shawl one of the women had made. The soft pastels blended together like a gorgeous sunrise so unlike the shawl she had seen one of the women from Hag Hallow wear at the store.

From a distance it had looked kinda cool, but when she had sidled closer to see the pattern, she had been startled to see it was nothing but skulls strung together. It had made her shudder and she had beat a hasty retreat.

Why would anyone even wear that unless they were witches? Confusion flooded in as she tried to figure out what was really going on with those women. Most everyone in the church did business with them and people like Pam, Alan, Dawna, and even the pastor kept telling her they were weird but harmless. She guessed they should know as most of them had lived their whole lives in Totem and she had only been here five years, but then there were the stories she had heard from other members of the congregation, especially about the mother of the lady who owned the plant shop. Some of the elderly ones, like Miss Kepler, were completely convinced that the woman had been a witch. So if the mother had been a witch, was her daughter? And her daughter's friends?

She suddenly flashed back to her aunt rambling on about some woman named Ellen? Elizabeth? Eleanora, that was it. Was that the same person? She tried to remember what was said, but her aunt babbled on endlessly about everything and Mona had learned to listen with half an ear, her thoughts usually someplace else.

She furrowed her brow. She wished she knew more about witches so she could be sure she was protecting herself from them. How would you even know somebody was a witch? From what she had seen, the women always dressed pretty much like everyone in town with jeans and tee-shirts, except for the one with the dreadlocks. She usually wore flowy dresses and weird necklaces with rocks, shells, and sometimes even sticks dangling from them.

She had tried to talk to Pastor Barnwell about it, but each time she brought it up, he just got irritated so she stopped. The old ladies at church seemed to know about the dead mother but they just exchanged looks when she had tried to ask questions about the women in the hollow and changed the subject.

Maybe if she looked online, she could find some information that would help her figure things out.

Stuffing her crochet back in the bag, she moved from the recliner to the couch, where her elderly laptop rested among piles of church programs and Christian-themed magazines. Turning it on, she sat back as it went through prolonged whirring before the screen lit up. Tapping the Google icon, she typed in the word "witch". She stared at the bewildering number of witch-related topics that appeared. She moved the cursor around, hovering over one and then another. Suddenly, she was struck with the idea that maybe even looking up information would be like touching something evil. She hastily closed the tab.

Chapter Nine

Light was just edging its way around the curtains in her bedroom when Dawna rolled onto her back and opened her eyes. Normally, she would turn on the light and then, after a trip to the bathroom, settle in her little recliner to read from the Bible before checking the calendar on her phone and praying over the day's schedule.

Today, she couldn't muster the energy to get out from under the heavy blanket of disappointment and duty lying on her heart. When she felt the pressure of a potential migraine beginning to build behind her eyes, she forced herself to the bathroom to swallow medication to ward off the worst of its effects. Settling into her chair, her hand hovered over the Bible before reaching beyond it to pick up her smartphone. Closing one eye so she could focus, she pulled up the day's calendar. There was a budget meeting for the women's part of the revival followed by a meeting to schedule church events for the next quarter, and then the weekly card writing for birthdays and such.

Revulsion rose out of her mid-section. She couldn't do it; wouldn't do it. She would plead her migraine and not do it. Caleb wouldn't be happy, but she didn't care what Caleb thought. She needed some time to hide away from all the responsibilities she carried.

Both eyes popped open when she realized that it wasn't just a small rebellious thought about caring what Caleb thought; she really didn't care. It startled her. The grumbling in her heart was getting more vocal. She felt movement and changes deep inside her that she didn't understand but were definitely there. She really needed some quiet time to sort out her emotions. She lifted her phone again and scrolled to her contacts. Then punched the number to the church secretary although she knew Pam would not be in the office for several more hours.

When the answering machine kicked on, she spoke after the message had ended and it beeped. "Hey, Pam. This is Dawna. I have one of my migraines so I won't be able to come in today. Tell everyone I'll catch up with them tomorrow. Thanks." Clicking off, she went back to bed.

She was dozing fitfully when Caleb stuck his head around the door. "Hey, you've overslept."

Dawna shielded her eyes with her hand. "I have a migraine," she whispered.

"Geez, you have lousy timing. You know how busy this time of year is. You need to pull yourself together and try to make it." The door shut just shy of a slam.

Turning her head into her pillow angry, hurt tears flowed.

The medication subverted the migraine's blossoming and a shower did the rest by mid-morning. Dawna dressed, knowing she could pick up her schedule without much inconvenience to anyone. She dressed for church business, modestly making up her face and styling her short bob.

Gathering up her notebooks, folders, and purse, she headed out to resume her role as the perfect pastor's wife, but the car didn't turn toward the church. Instead she found herself driving in the opposite direction to the little cemetery on the backside of town. Although maintained, it wasn't used anymore. There were few unfilled plots remaining so the city had closed it years ago and opened a new one north of town.

She pulled into the small parking area and got out. Sun filtered through the old Douglas firs standing sentinel over the inhabitants and there was an early summer warmth in the air. Gravel crunched under her shoes as she headed to the little marble memorial bench sitting at the edge of the grounds. It was constantly in danger of being overtaken by the laurel growing behind it, but so far the city maintenance crew was keeping the towering bush in abeyance. Urns, on either side, had not survived the decades of changing weather, and were little more than the bases now. Sinking into the shadows, a cool gentle breeze stroked her temples as she gazed out at the jumble of grave markers. She felt her spirit quieting. The dead held no expectations of her and she was grateful.

She was startled to hear tires turning into the tiny parking area. It was the first time in her escapes to the cemetery anyone else had come. Suddenly she felt vulnerable. Grabbing the handles of her purse, she prepared for flight from the bench when the vehicle's occupant strode into view. It was Felicity Sewell from the deli carrying a bouquet and a bag in her hands. She moved purposely among the headstones.

Finally she stopped and stared seemingly at the ground before squatting down. Felicity reached into the bag to pull out a cloth, carefully wiping off an unseen grave marker. When finished, she laid the bouquet on the grave before touching her fingers to her lips and placing them on the headstone.

When Felicity had returned to her car and Dawna had heard it turn out of the short drive onto the street, she got up to cross to the place Felicity had been.

A shaggy, unconventional collection of leaves, grasses and a few wild flowers rested near the plain concrete headstone. The name on it was Duane Joseph Sewell and it was dated 1946 – 1969. Staring at it, she remembered vaguely being told at some time or another that Felicity had a brother who had been killed in an accident years ago. This must be him. While most of the grave markers were coved in moss, lichen and mold, the fact that Duane's was so well cared for indicated that Felicity must come often to visit her brother.

What would it be like to be as loved in life as he apparently was in death?

***

Driving back to the deli, Felicity reflected on seeing Dawna's car at the cemetery. She hadn't spotted the woman until she was leaving, hidden as she was by the shadows over the old Morgan memorial bench. They seldom spoke when meeting publicly other than when Dawna would pick up something from the deli so Felicity felt no obligation to acknowledge her presence in the cemetery. Something sparked in her brain as she thought about Dawna. In all the years she had owned the deli, she had seen virtually everyone from the church on any number of occasions. Everyone except Caleb. She did not remember a time he had ever come in. When she prepared food for the different church meetings, it was always Pam, Dawna, even Mona who picked up the order. She realized he would even avoid her if they happened to cross paths doing other business. Funny, she had never paid attention to that before. Maybe because she didn't really care. Holier-than-thou Caleb was not someone she made room for on her radar.

***

Glancing at her watch, Dawna realized she would be able to make the second meeting scheduled for today. Although she was tempted to continue with her migraine story, guilt swamped the idea and she dutifully turned toward the church after pulling out of the cemetery parking lot. A funk settled over her so even the sunny day seemed to darken as she got closer to her destination. When had the bright hope of living a life of faith shriveled into the dry desert of endless obligation?

Pam was handing around copies of the fall/winter calendar pages when she entered the fellowship hall. "Dawna!" she said. "Are you all right to be here?"

Dawna forced a cheery smile and nodded. "Yes. I caught it early enough, my medication was able to get it under control."

Although nearly the same age as Dawna, Pam always assumed a motherly role with her. Pam's own mother had served as the secretary for the church for decades before her vision had deteriorated to the point she had to give it up. Pam had helped her, more and more frequently, as her eyesight worsened, so it seemed natural for Pam to slide into the job when her mother had retired.

Dawna looked around the table, noting there seemed to be fewer women than usual. Doing a mental roll call, she ticked off Bethany, Nan, Pam, and Mona. They were missing two members of the committee. "Where's Trina and Marsha?" she asked.

"Marsha went to the Valley for a few weeks. Her granddaughter is having heart surgery to fix that hole she was born with and Marsha wants to be there to help out," Pam said before glancing at Nan. "Trina? I don't know."

Everyone also looked at Trina's mother. Her expression was somewhere between exasperated and embarrassed. She let out a sigh. "Trina has decided to drop out for the time being," she said in answer to the unspoken question from the other women.

"Why?" Mona gasped.

"She said she doesn't believe the only way women get to heaven is through the kitchen or the nursery."

Dawna stared at her. "Okay, I'm confused."

"She says," Nan continued with a slight shake in her voice, "that the only role for women here is to serve the church itself and, by that, she actually means the men of the church. She said we don't do anything to help the community outside ourselves and that we exist only to make the pastor look good."

Nan stopped abruptly and flushed, "I'm sorry, Dawna. I shouldn't have repeated that part of our argument. Forgive me."

Dawna shook her head. "No forgiveness needed, Nan. She's not wrong."

Chapter Ten

"But we do lots for the community," Mona burst out. "We make those lap robes, shawls, and stuff in Circle. And the food boxes at Thanksgiving and the toy drive at Christmas."

"Yes, we do," Nan said. "But as Trina pointed out in our disagreement, nobody from the church actually delivers them. We schlep them over to St. Bartholomew's and let our Catholic brethren be the ones to actually step into people's messy, problematic lives. We stay a safe, sanitary arm's length away from the dirty work of dealing with people whose needs would put a light on, and I quote, 'our hide-bound insularity'."

As an awkward silence settled over the group, Pam idly ruffled the paper-clipped pages of the calendar with her thumb. "You know, every year all I do is move the same events to the appropriate date. There is nothing in these pages that the church hasn't done since I was a girl."

"It's odd, now that I think about it, but Alan and I do a lot in the community and not one bit of it is through the church," Bethany said.

"Well, that's kinda what businesses do, isn't it. Like advertising to get more customers?" Mona asked, thinking of the Little Leaguers, she had seen around town, sporting neon green tee-shirts with Newton Insurance Agency printed on the back.

"No, Mona, it's not. Believe what you will, but Alan and I don't care if we ever get a customer from our community service. We do it because a very long time ago someone was there for us when we were going through the worst moment of our lives and we vowed afterward to try and follow their example to do the same for others."

"Would you care to share?" Dawna asked quietly. "Unless you feel it's too personal."

Bethany slowly moved the handle on her coffee cup from her right hand to her left hand and back as she looked into the past. "When Alan and I were starting the insurance agency, we were dead broke. I mean like sometimes us not eating so we could feed Nate and Cindy. Before we could even get a toe-hold on surviving, there came the winter of that terrible flu which was hitting and taking children far oftener than adults. Nate caught it and he was so, so sick.

"There wasn't a doctor in town since old Doc Devers had had a stroke and shut his practice down. Alan and I dug through every pocket, the couch, the car to try to find enough change to buy gas to get him into the Valley for help. We came up with enough to maybe buy a bottle of baby aspirin. With no gas to even drive to the store, I walked through the pouring rain to what is now Seb's grocery, terrified my son would be gone before I got back home.

"When I got to the medication aisle, I realized I was a nickel short of even being able to buy the smallest bottle. Standing there with the package in my hand, I honestly considered stealing it. That I would even have to think of such a thing just broke me. I was so exhausted from staying up with him around the clock for two days, so cold from the stormy walk, and so shamed by our inability to do what we needed to do to save him.

"Then someone wrapped me in the warmest, most empathetic hug I have ever had in my life. She whispered 'Tell me' and I did. Every wretched detail." Bethany paused as the emotions tied to the memory momentarily swamped her.

The other women shot irritated looks at Mona who blurted out, "Who was it?"

Bethany looked steadily at Mona before answering her. "It was Ophelia Swanner."

Mona's mouth opened in surprise. "The witch!"

Nan snorted. "Geez, Mona, give that up, will you?"

"You know, Mona, at that moment I think I would have accepted help from the devil himself, I was that desperate. Anyway, she put the aspirin on back on the shelf telling me she had what Nate needed.

"She drove me home and then called her mom. In what seemed like no time, Felicity showed up carrying some of those brown bottles and blue jars that Eleanora always used for her concoctions. I suppose Alan and I should have protested but, honestly, we had nothing left to even whimper with.

"They rubbed a salve on Nate's back and chest, then gave him some drops out of a couple of bottles." She closed her eyes. "I still remember the smells. The salve was green and astringent. The drops were warm and faintly peppery.

Within an hour, Nate's fever broke and he was barely coughing. He was finally able to sleep. We put him between us, and we all, even tiny Cindy, slept like the dead.

"In the morning, he was hungry and, while not completely back to his normal energy level, obviously on the mend. When I went to the kitchen to see what I might be able to find for him, I found the counter loaded with jars of canned vegetables, fruits, jams, and homemade bread. There were eggs and goat's milk in the refrigerator. And there was a note." A small smile formed on her lips. "I still have it. In fact, it's framed in Alan's office so we would never forget the hands that came out of a very dark night to help us."

"What did it say?" Mona asked as the air of hushed expectancy grew thick over the table.

"Mona, it's possible Bethany may not want to share," Dawna said.

"No, no. It's fine. Many people have seen it over the years. It said 'I have looked ahead and see all will be well.' It was signed with an old-school E. And she was right, it was."

"Eleanora?" Nan asked. "I never met her, but I have heard stories about her. Apparently, she had a gift."

"Yes," Bethany nodded. "She had a gift. Years and years later, Ophelia told Alan it was no accident she had been at the store that night. She said her mother sent her and told her to look around for someone who was in terrible distress."

"How'd she know?" Mona asked. "Did someone else tell her?"

"Absolutely not. No one knew what was going on except Alan and I."

"So this lady knew without anyone telling her? That's spooky. Like witchcraft, maybe."

"You know, Mona," Dawna said through clenched teeth. "the Bible is full of stories about visions, dreams, prophesy; even visitations."

"But that stuff doesn't happen anymore."

"I don't recall any place in the Bible that says those forms of communication would no longer happen once we got cell phones," Nan said. "Maybe it's more like we have forgotten how to look for and believe in such things."

Before Mona could speak again, Dawna asked the group. "Do we want to do the same drill we have done forever, or do we want to explore ways we could extend our reach beyond the quarterly tea in September?"

Anxiousness gripped Mona. She desperately needed to be safely wrapped in the steady flow of calendar events the church followed year after year. But she sensed an undercurrent rippling through the women around her that she couldn't decipher. "I like the teas," she said.

Bethany looked thoughtful. "I, for one, would like to see us do more outreach and involvement in the community." There was a murmur of assent among the other women.

"But exactly what and how are we going to do that?" Pam asked. "I am totally onboard with the idea but shouldn't we have some idea of what we can do to be of real service and how we can go about doing it?"

"We should," Dawna agreed. "And I think the best place to start is to seek direction from people who have been doing it for decades."

"Like another church?" Mona asked.

Dawna shook her head. "Like the Hag Hallow ladies."

Mona's mouth opened and closed like a gaping fish. "That wouldn't be right. They're..." She stopped short of finishing her sentence when Nan growled at her.

"You know, Mona, those women have been practicing what we preach for a very long time. I concur with Dawna. I think that is a very good place to get a handle on what we can do to be of actual service to the community," Bethany said.

"But what about Pastor Barnwell? I don't think he likes them at all."

"This is the women's group and I, for one, don't care what Caleb thinks," Dawna said crisply.

Chapter Eleven

Felicity used the usually quiet hours between the lunch trade and the early dinner pickups as her time to prep for the next day and to prepare dinner when it was her night to feed everyone. She peeked out of the miniscule kitchen when she heard the door open, expecting one of the property's occupants. She was startled to see Dawna Barnwell approach the counter.

She came out, wiping her hands on a towel. "Oh my, Dawna, did I forget an order?"

Dawna shook her head. "No, no." She paused a moment before saying, "I was just wondering when you might have a few minutes to talk." Her nervousness was palpable.

"Now actually works fine," she answered. "Just let me pop the potato salad in the refrigerator. Would you like a cup of tea? I have some of the honey lavender you like."

"Yes. That would be lovely."

It will also help calm your nerves, Felicity thought as she filled a small teapot with hot water and plucked a teabag from the little rack next to the coffeemaker. She carried the saucer holding the teapot and a cup to the table at the rear where Evan and Trey usually sat. Setting it down, she motioned to Dawna. "Let me grab a cup of coffee and we can sit here. It's the most private table in the deli."

Without actually meeting her eyes, Dawna nodded. As Felicity fetched her cup of coffee, she observed the slight hesitation before the woman took herself to the table. There was obvious ambivalence at play.

Dawna had opened the teabag's packaging and dropped the bag into the steaming pot by the time Felicity joined her.

Dawna stared at the steeping tea before speaking. "First of all, I want to apologize for the way I and others have treated you and the rest of the women here through the years. Our—no—my actions have been very uncharitable. I have let the views and beliefs of others determine the window through which I judged and acted toward many things for a very long time." She kept her eyes lowered before turning to look out the window. Several silent minutes passed before she spoke again. "This is a very peaceful place, isn't it?"

"Yes. That was one of the intentions guiding us as we cleansed the land and rebuilt it for a better purpose."

Dawna looked back at her curiously. "Cleansed the land?"

Felicity now looked out the window. "There were many old sins and ghosts of bad acts resting here. We spent much time rooting them out and replenishing the good that is inherent in the earth."

The only image of cleansing Dawna was able to summon was of her husband waving his hands around while proclaiming he was cleansing the parishioners of their sins. Her puzzlement showed.

"Ophelia's mother possessed an uncanny understanding of the ways of nature, and she passed that knowledge on to her daughter and, to a certain extent me, as I practically lived there when I was growing up. Becca literally grew up on this land. It has always been as much a part of her as her breathing."

"I'm sorry. I'm still not sure what you're talking about."

"Let's just say the land told us what it needed and we complied."

Though still not understanding, Dawna nonetheless nodded as she poured tea into her cup. She took a sip before speaking. "You mentioned Ophelia. Apparently, you and she were of service to Alan and Bethany Newton a very long time ago."

"They're good people. They contribute a great deal to the community."

"Yes, they do," Dawna agreed. "And that is why I am here. Recent discussions among our women's group has illuminated the fact that our church actually does very little in the community at large. To repeat something that was quoted, it seems we have a 'hide-bound insularity'. We want to change that."

Felicity nodded and it was now her turn to look puzzled. "That sounds like an excellent idea. There are a lot of needs here in Totem."

"Yes, I suspect there are." Dawna now looked steadily at Felicity. "The very sad problem is we don't know how to identify them, let alone help. We need guidance and direction and I guess that's why I'm here."

Felicity recognized there was something deeper going on personally with Dawna. Surely, the women's group was capable of figuring out things like food boxes, shut-in visitation, meeting transportation needs. All they had to do was look at St. Bartholomew's community outreach.

Fractures in Dawna's long-lived façade opened and her face abruptly crumpled. "Actually, I don't even know why I'm here. After decades of being so sure of myself and my faith, I have lost sight of both. When I saw you the other day at the cemetery, I saw someone who seemed to be standing on solid ground with herself while I'm flailing around in the quicksand." She paused to dig a tissue out of her purse and dab at her eyes. "I'm sorry. I don't even know where that came from."

"It a cry for help from the real Dawna hidden deep within you. I think that Dawna is tired of living in Caleb's no-doubt-demanding shadow. Of meeting the expectations of a judgmental congregation. Of only being allowed to tap into the smallest, shallowest part of her true ability. Of being forced to live in the straitjacket of man's image instead of her own expansive feminine nature."

Felicity's words rang through her like a clear, pealing bell. It felt like her soul literally lunged toward them shouting yes, yes, yes. The strength of the emotion suddenly surging through her was frightening. She became aware that the little rebellion that had been rattling in the background had just moved closer to the surface.

Felicity leaned across the table to cup Dawna's hands in her own. "There are many ways to serve, but the best way is through the truest part of yourself. That is the part you must find and uncover. We can help but only when you are sure you wish to peer though doors of possibility other than what you've looked through for most of your life."

"I'm scared," Dawna whispered. "It might change everything."

"Not might, but will. The authentic Dawna will not likely be the false-front who goes to church every Sunday and presides over endless insipid meetings. It will be a person who is fully in her own power; not someone trying desperately to see herself in the reflection of someone else."

"I'm not sure I would even know how to do that."

Felicity smiled. "I think you do or you would not be sitting across this table from me right now. I think it's time that you honored your own feelings, thoughts, and questions instead of sublimating or denying them. I think it's time you honored yourself."

Dawna nodded uncertainly. As much as she craved the sentiment in Felicity's words, it was in direct conflict with what she had been taught her whole life—that she was secondary to the needs and demands of both the church and her husband.

Although Felicity had seen a surge of boldness in Dawna's aura during their conversation, she now saw it dissipating. The woman across from her was withdrawing back into the Dawna she had always known

"I need to go. Caleb has a revival meeting tonight and he's going to want his dinner," Dawna said as she pulled her purse into her lap. "I appreciate you taking the time for me. How much do I owe you for the tea?"

Felicity shook her head. "No charge and we're here whenever you might need to talk again." She stood up when Dawna slid out of her chair and started for the door only to stop when Felicity spoke again.

When she looked back, Felicity asked her. "Dawna, what if God were a woman?"

Chapter Twelve

"You know Caleb will go absolutely ballistic," Ophelia said. "He has never forgiven my mother, and by extension me, for that dust-up when he first took over pastoring the church. He thinks we're attempting to influence Dawna, the shit's gonna be flying."

"Ummm, let me try to remember who, in the not too distant past, predicted a shit storm was heading our way," Jan said, reaching for more crackers to crumble in her salmon chowder.

"The impression I got when I was casting was that it would be something we would have no control over. You know, like Evan and Trey just sort of happening out of the blue. Not something we would deliberately conjure up ourselves."

"But we aren't conjuring," Becca noted. "We had no hand in the fact Dawna shows up here ostensibly to find out how to help the community. From what Felicity said, it sounds like Dawna is really searching for something and for some reason felt compelled to come here."

"There is a certain synchronicity to it," Felicity agreed. "I've visited Duane every week for fifty years and rarely have seen anyone else at the cemetery. Then this week, there's Dawna sitting on the old memorial bench."

"And later she shows up actually wanting to talk to you," Jan said. "Yup, sounds like storm clouds, not of our doing, are beginning to gather."

"And what can Caleb do to us anyway? Try to ruin our reputations? Seriously, banana slugs are thought of more highly than we are in this town," Ophelia noted.

"Good point," Jan nodded.

"Do you think she'll come back, other than to pick up food?" Becca asked.

Felicity shrugged. "I don't know. She really is balancing on the edge. She is not a happy woman, and she knows it. But is she unhappy enough to try to find a way to something that fits her heart and soul better, or will she just add some do-gooding as a way to glue the surface she has maintained for decades back together?"

"I guess we just wait and see," Becca said.

"You know she's coming back, and with her, the storm," Ophelia said cheerfully.

The other three looked at her. They knew Eleanora had passed more than just earth knowledge along to her daughter. And, truthfully, it could get danged annoying at times.

Becca sighed deeply. "Unicorns would be nice just once."

***

The anxiousness Mona carried back from the church meeting did not dissipate when she picked up her dinner from the Burger Hut. The hamburger that had tasted so good was now sitting heavy in her stomach. She dutifully did her nightly Bible reading. However, if the meaning of much of the verses escaped her before, tonight it was as though she hadn't actually read them at all. She never could figure out what the Old Testament was talking about with all those ancient laws and long lists of people who couldn't have mattered much since they just showed up as a bunch of unpronounceable names. She liked the New Testament better. Pastor Barnwell used a lot of the verses in his sermons and she loved discovering them in her reading. It always felt like another way of gaining his approval. The Psalms were her favorite. They were usually short and kinda like pretty word poems.

Although she had actually finished the daily readings, the Bible sat open in her ample lap while she thought about the meeting. She didn't understand why the other women were thinking of changing things. She hated change. Even when her elderly, demanding aunt that she had cared for died, she wasn't relieved to be free of the endless belittling she had been subjected to. She was deeply anxious and frustrated for a long time. She struggled to order the hours so she was comfortably safe in a known routine again. When she was offered the job of cleaning the church twice a week, it had provided her with a means to anchor her days. Over time, she had been invited to join several of the groups and her world had settled into a safe circle of known activities. Now the women wanted to mess that all up.

She struggled when taking on new and unfamiliar tasks so the things she was given to do when preparing for the various occasions were never very difficult. It was hard for her to get her head around complex tasks. She always got herself into a muddle and one of the other women would have to bail her out. But she was happy when she could set tables, carry plates, hand out programs, help clean up after. Pastor Barnwell always complimented her on how good she was at her assigned job.

She couldn't understand why the women would even want to deal with people outside the church. She herself didn't really like other people. They were always doing and saying things that confused her. She didn't even like it very much when someone new came to the church. She always made sure to carefully avoid them until she saw how others interacted with the new people.

Her mind jumped to Dawna saying she didn't care what Pastor Barnwell thought. She was completely perplexed by the very idea. Pastor Barnwell was such a good man it felt like a sin to speak against him. Why would his wife even consider doing things that might upset him?

And why was everyone always getting irritated with her when she talked about the witches? Miss Kepler seemed sure they were witches and she had been part of the church longer than anyone, even Pastor Barnwell. Bethany and Nan had said that person, she forgot who, had ways of knowing things without anyone telling her. Wasn't that something witches could do?

And Dawna said to everyone she was going to see the Hag Hallow women. Why would she risk that? Pastor Barnwell didn't like those women at all. It would make him unhappy if he thought anyone in the church did more than sometimes pick up food from the deli.

Something unpleasant was jittering through her body. She struggled to try to put the pieces of information floating around in her brain together, but as soon as she focused on one, others would slip away. All she knew for sure was she felt like something bad was coming and she was pretty sure the Hag Hallow women were making it happen.

***

Dawna had carefully kept her thoughts in neutral as she fed Caleb and got him off to his meeting. When he had perfunctorily asked how the women's meeting had gone, she knew a simple 'fine' would satisfy him. He actually didn't care what went on in their meetings as long as what he expected of them was accomplished.

After tidying up the kitchen, Dawna fixed herself a cup of tea to take to her study. Only when she was settled in her chair did she turn her full attention to focusing on and picking through her short conversation with Felicity.

She wondered at herself for blurting out something as personal as her current spiritual state. She had learned long ago to keep a lot of information close to her, expressing only those things acceptable in polite company or expected of her in her role as the pastor's wife.

And why had she not noticed, despite her many trips to pick up food, the deep sense of peace and safety that almost literally hung in the air where the deli was situated? Was sitting there, actually taking it in, what triggered her divulgence?

Or was it Felicity herself? Dawna knew she had always exhibited her stern judgment of the Hag Hallow women when she happened into their presence, yet, despite decades of being borderline rude, she had felt absolutely no animosity from Felicity, only a quiet curiosity. She had been treated with grace and kindness. There had been no measuring or judgment. Somehow she felt if she had blurted out the most heinous of secrets, Felicity would not have found her abhorrent.

Where did that come from in the woman? Dawna wrinkled her brow as she tried to remember what she had been told about Felicity's past. Her mother had run a tiny bakery and catering business which the oldest church members still talked about with great fondness. There had been Felicity and her older brother. She didn't recall anyone mentioning the father so she guessed that he had been out of the picture very long ago, for whatever reason. Apparently the mother died of breast cancer when Felicity was in her mid-teens. She then came under the care of her brother, who was a contemporary of Caleb's. The few mentions of him were always preceded by 'not to speak ill of the dead' so he must have had something of a reputation in Totem. She had married someone right out of high school who abandoned her shortly after her brother had died.

So much tragedy piled on when someone was so young. How do you survive all that?

Dawna saw what a state of grace she had been allowed to live in. Her own parents, although quite elderly, were safely ensconced in a nice assistive living facility. While she had no brothers, both her sisters were comfortable and planning for their retirements. Her nieces and nephews seemed to be getting along in their lives well. She herself had lived a very safe life in the confines of the church and Totem.

And now she felt the urge to blow that all up to feed some indefinable hunger gnawing at her.

Her thoughts finally circled to the question Felicity had asked her as she was leaving the deli. What if God was a woman? The mere thought felt blasphemous and yet, even as she felt repelled by the concept, it also attracted her.

She knew all the words in the Bible referencing God were masculine. Closing her eyes, she dug back into what she had learned in Bible College. She remembered while the terms relating to God directly were masculine, the original Hebrew used the feminine in reference to the Holy Spirit. A brisk discussion broke out as the male students took issue with the budding feminists who demanded to know why they had a problem with there being a feminine side to the Triune God. She had been embarrassed by how militant some of the girls had been in their arguments. She remembered sitting at her desk with her head down and thinking, "That's not how godly women are supposed to behave."

Dawna sat forward. She had just stumbled on the mantra of her life. "That's not how godly women are supposed to behave." Who created the rules marking the path she had walked since her youth? Who benefitted from her struggle to never put a foot wrong and be willing to meekly accept chastisement when she did? Whose expectations was she struggling to meet?

A wash of memories from the many, many workshops and retreats she had attended through the decades streamed past her mental eyes. How to keep the parsonage prepared for unexpected visitors. How to present yourself modestly. How to support your husband's pastoral work. How to organize meetings and facilitate groups. Lord, it was all milk and pap. Where was the Biblical meat for women?

Something long, long tamped down began to push its way up amongst her darting thoughts.

She, too, had gone to Bible college. She had taken the same classes as Caleb; participated in the same programs and missions; graduated with the same degree. In fact, that was where they had met and eventually become engaged. They married a few months following graduation after Caleb had received his first call to pastor.

From the time Caleb had put the engagement ring on her finger, she had envisioned them working as equal partners in doing the Lord's work, but somewhere through the years she had been shunted off onto a different track, leaving her farther and farther from being of real service.

How odd. The Hag Hallow women, who followed no man, were seemingly much more aligned in their service with the Bible's dictates than the women in her church.

Her nerves suddenly felt electrified. Followed no man began to loop through her thoughts. Each repeat opened more of a desperate hunger for the space it implied.

Chapter Thirteen

Cars began to turn into the wide graveled parking lot; each disgorging one or more women.

"Time to make ourselves scarce," Trey rumbled as Evan walked past his cabin.

"You're welcome to come up to the gardens and hang out with me," Evan said. "It's kinda my go-to place for these things. Felicity always sends up a thermos of coffee and a sack lunch."

Trey spent a moment weighing his options. He had already explored the town he no longer knew with two exceptions. Man, he had spent half a century running and he still couldn't face some facts.

And he was tired. He wasn't even sure he had it in him today to push the bike out, let alone kick it to life, and ride. This morning he could almost feel the terminus of his life drifting through the small cabin.

A fear of being alone when the inevitable end came was steeping in him. "If you don't mind the company, I'd sure appreciate it."

"Let me grab the stuff at the deli and I'll meet you by the path."

Setting the bucket he was carrying at the base of the path, Evan turned back toward the deli. Felicity spotted him striding by the window and sat two white bags on the counter next to the big Stanley® thermos.

"Hey, Evan, would you mind taking one of these to Trey? I was going to have Enoch do it, but Becca has already snagged him to help out at the workshop."

"No problem. I'm dragging him up to the gardens with me, at least for a while."

In answer, Felicity turned and pulled one of the to-go cups off the stack, putting some sugar and creamer packets in it along with a stirrer before adding it to one of the bags. "You'll need an extra cup then."

Trey was waiting, his guitar in one hand. "What's with the little flags?" he asked gesturing to the few remaining in the bucket.

Evan sat the thermos inside the bucket before collecting it. "Becca marks the plants that are mature enough to harvest for her wild crafting class. It protects those not ready for harvest and keeps the ladies from picking something they shouldn't."

"You ever seen any men at these things the gals are always putting on?"

Evan shook his head. "Nope. Just women."

"Wonder why that is?" Trey said. He stopped part-way up the path to draw some deep, wheezy breaths. "Damn, don't remember this being so steep back then."

"Maybe it would help if you used the handrail," Evan said, gesturing to the project he had recently completed.

His thought had been that, although still very active and mobile, the women were getting older and it would be a way to prevent a fall as they went up and down to the garden beds. He had had a bit of tussle with Ophelia and Becca about installing it. He had actually wanted to dig out and put in tiered steps similar to those leading to the women's cabins, but Ophelia squashed the idea when she asked how they would get the garden cart up and down. The compromise was the handrail. Of course, so far the women had carefully avoided using it as if it served as a reminder of their waning physicality.

Trey took hold of it and began to lever himself up the path. "Was a time I could make this drunk and stoned," he said. "Used to be one of Calhoun's shacks he passed off as a cabin up here. Great place for the bad kids of Totem to party."

Once they reached the top, Trey stopped. "Whoa. This is some layout," he said, looking around at the greenhouses, the various beds and the couple of small hoop houses used for drying Ophelia's herbs and medicine plants. He eased himself down on the log bench beside the door to one of the greenhouses.

Returning from putting the bucket away, Evan turned on the soaker hoses before checking the thermometers in the greenhouses. Coming back out, he zipped open some of the covers allowing air to circulate so they wouldn't overheat. Trey was strumming an old song from the '60s, singing along to his playing.

Although age and lifestyle had roughened his voice, it made a pleasant background to Evan's various chores. Eventually a rumble in his stomach made him glance at his watch.

Trey had moved to a bench on the shady side of the greenhouse, taking the lunch bags with him. "Hungry?" Evan asked.

Trey set his guitar aside. "Enough to take a bite out of a skunk butt."

"There's a cup in one of those," Evan said as he twisted the cap off the thermos. The two men ate and drank in a companionable silence. When finished, Evan balled up the bags and wrappers before pitching them in the old burn barrel on the edge of the medicinal bed.

Returning, he divvied up the last of the coffee. Trey tore open a sugar packet. "So what's your story, Hjort?" he asked as he shook it into his cup.

"What'd you mean?"

"Well, you know that I'm a worthless drifter who spent my life riding the roads looking for something I never found. From what I've seen, you have a good education. Some of those shirts you wear look like they cost a pretty penny at one time. So how did you manage to end up here hauling bark dust around for the gals?"

Evan stared out at the forest surrounding the garden area. "Maybe because I was so busy keeping my eye on chasing the almighty dollar, I missed seeing that it was poisoning everything around me. Woke up one day to divorce papers and a business teetering on the edge of bankruptcy through the mismanagement of a partner I trusted. What remained after I got the business squared away and shut down, the wife got in the divorce settlement. Nothing left for me there, so like you, I just got in my van and hit the road."

"So you went one way in life and I went another and we ended up at the same place is what you're saying."

"Pretty much," Evan said.

"So where are you going from here?"

"Not sure. The old ego got pretty much pulverized the last couple of years. Makes you question every decision you ever made or might make."

Trey's voice was quiet. "Pretty sure I made every bad decision in the book and now I guess I've made about my last decision in coming back," he said. "Used up everything I got. Just the dregs waiting for the call yonder."

A darker silence stretched between the men again.

Trey broke it. "Would you be willing to do me a favor, Hjort? When my time comes would you ask Felicity if she would bury me with Duane? Maybe, despite me being nothing but a raggedy old sinner, the Good Lord will see fit to let us hang out together."

Evan glanced at the man's weathered red face. "If I'm still here, I'll do that."

Something in Trey's face relaxed. "Got a funeral plan. Cremation. The papers are in my saddlebag. Make sure she knows about that, too."

"You could tell her yourself."

"Nah. Ain't comfortable putting that on her while I'm still kicking. But maybe when I'm gone, she'll be able to forgive me enough to do it if someone else asks for me."

A feeling of foreboding washed through Evan. It was only a couple more months before the women's 'busy season' finished and he would be hitting the road. Trey was talking like that was more than enough time for him to act on the man's request.

Their reverie was broken by Enoch's voice. "Mister? Mister?"

Evan got up from the bench to circle to the front of the greenhouse. "Hey, Enoch."

He could tell the man was flustered at not seeing them as soon as he had climbed the path. Mimicking what he had observed the women do in their interactions with him, Evan stood quiet.

Enoch's mouth worked silently as he struggled to order what he wanted to relay to Evan. "Miss Becca…," he started then paused before starting again. "Miss Becca say three." He stopped again as he again carefully focused on the relayed message. "Yes. She say that. Three."

"Three it is. Thank you, Enoch. Tell her okay."

The man repeated it. "Okay."

"Yes. Okay."

Enoch stood a moment before nodding and turning to head back down the small hill.

Evan watched until he saw Enoch reach the parking and turn toward the path passing the cabins as it headed to the gazebo area where the women held their various classes and events. Returning to the bench he picked up his now cool coffee.

"So what's the story with that guy?" Trey asked.

"Apparently the women kinda adopted him years ago. Jan said it was shortly after she joined up with them."

"What'd they do? Pick him up off the side of the road?"

"Almost," Evan said. "According to what Jan told me, Enoch's parents were some of those back-to-earthers. Bought a little farm somewhere close by. Had a couple of kids when they showed up and a couple of more while they were here. Enoch was the last one.

"Apparently they didn't believe in doctors and stuff like that too much. Midwife delivered Enoch but they didn't do the PKU test they usually do on all newborns. Enoch had the genetic disorder which meant, according to Jan, he wasn't able to process certain amino acids from what he ate so they built up a toxicity that led to his mental disability."

"So how'd he end up here?"

"It seems that when the older kids grew up, the parents up and sold their farm and moved away, leaving Enoch behind like some unwanted dog. Man couldn't care for himself so he took to going back to the farm or to a few other places he was able to remember. Needless to say, everyone chased him away. Finally, somebody called the police. They apparently tried to get some of the churches involved, but they weren't about to take on the lifetime project Enoch represented. The chief was trying to arrange for the state to take him when the women got wind of the situation. They barreled in on the police, who had been letting Enoch sleep in the town's jail cell…"

"Yup, I know the place. Slept off a few nights there myself," Trey interjected.

"Anyway, they talked the chief out of getting the state involved and took over on him themselves. Now he lives in that little travel trailer with the women carefully feeding him foods that won't worsen his condition. They've taught him some skills so he spends his days helping them out with simple tasks."

"They sure have a penchant for taking in society's roadkill. Enoch, you, me. Wonder what's in it for them?"

Evan shrugged. "Don't know. Felicity mentioned one time it had to do with some kind of rules they lived by. Don't really know what she meant."

"Well, for all their strange ways, they sure have done a fine job with the land." Trey stared across the gardens. "It's real peaceful now. A good place to die," he said softly.

Chapter Fourteen

Caleb woke up irritated. Alan had reported the evening before that the company from which they normally rented the tents for the revival had apparently shut up shop in the last year. He had researched some possible new rental places but knowing that what you see on the internet and what something really was could be worlds apart, he felt compelled to drive into the Valley and check things out in person. The revival was the one huge moneymaker of the year, and he couldn't risk ending up with something inadequate to house his show in.

He was settling the knot in his tie when he came into the kitchen. Dawna was just sliding his eggs onto a plate already containing toast and a sausage patty. For some reason the sight of her still in her bathrobe notched up his sense of being burdened.

She sat the plate on the kitchen island and turned to pour his coffee.

"Look, when you can finally get dressed, I need you to go to the church office and see if Pam comes in. This situation with her mother is beginning to get out of hand. She's taking so much time off; I'm thinking I might need to replace her."

"Her mother was diagnosed with the blood disorder just a few weeks ago. It's a pretty serious condition and I would think you might allow them time to get a treatment plan in order before deciding to kick them out. They've served the church for decades, longer even than you."

"It's their obligation to serve the church. And when they can't, other arrangements need to be made."

Caleb's cold answer ignited a torrent of rage-filled words Dawna almost couldn't stifle. How dare he act as though the only purpose for the two women's existence was to serve the church... his church? What was the church's obligation to them?

"Have a safe trip," she said mechanically through clenched teeth as she headed to her bedroom.

The cascading shower water did not lower the temperature of the scream inside her. Toweling off, she wanted nothing more than to shred every single thing in her life. A huge battle was being fought inside her. The Dawna who was so controlled and careful to always perform as expected was in combat with a side of her she had only recently glimpsed. A part of her wanting to call bullshit on everything in her life.

Long engrained habits led her to straighten her bedroom and tidy the kitchen before she headed to the church.

Although it was just striking the hour that Pam would have been unlocking the church office door, Dawna was surprised to see her already at her desk.

The woman did not look well with the dark circles under her eyes standing out sharply in her drawn face. The hostility Caleb's words had triggered swiftly dissipated. Pam's stress was palpable.

"Pam, I came to see what I could do to help," Dawna said, twisting the truth slightly.

Pam tapped the edge of a couple of file folders together on the desk, before slipping them into the desk drawer. "Thanks, Dawna, but I think I have everything caught up. Mom had a bad night. She finally went to sleep about two. Can't say I slept much better after that so I decided to come in and get caught up. We're meeting with the hematologist later today to see what the treatment plan is going to be. That should give me a better idea of when I might have to take off."

Dawna sat down in one of the two chairs in front of the desk. "Tell me what I can do to help."

Pam tried to arrange her face in a look of bright composure. "Oh, it will take a bit of juggling, but I think I can—" The mask of composure shattered. "Oh, god, this is so hard. I don't know how long, if ever, it will be for Mom's situation to be controlled. And I know this is the worst time of the year for me to have to constantly step out. And there's just me to be there for Mom. Bill's on the East Coast and, although he calls every day and has offered to send us money if we need it, he feels like he's being a rotten son because he isn't here to help so I have to spend time assuring him. And it's all happening during the worst time of the year and you know how Caleb is so picky about everything so I am scared to death that I am going to miss something or screw something up—" She abruptly dissolved into tears, something Dawna wasn't sure she had ever seen in all the years of their association.

Dawna got up to put her arms around Pam. Holding the shaking woman, she looked around the office and down the hall to the doors to Caleb's office, the fellowship hall, and the church nave itself. And although, she had passed through that corridor thousands of times in the many years that Caleb was pastor, she suddenly felt estranged from it all.

It was polished to a high shine thanks to Mona. She knew that beyond each of those doors everything was efficiently arranged and functioned well. But for the first time, she saw how sterile it was. No welcome or comfort hung in the air. It was as though the church worked hard to keep the messy part of its parishioners' lives at arm's length. She knew Caleb had never been comfortable in dealing with the emotional needs of people. He had honed his methods for deflecting them well. What was the point of everything here if there was nothing for the people?

Dawna squatted down so she was on eye level with Pam. "I want you to go home and take care of what you need to do there and do not worry about here. I can take care of it. When everything is more settled with your mother, then you can come back. Not until then."

"Dawna, that's too much to ask. You have so much on your plate already."

"No, Pam, I don't nearly have enough—of the right stuff."

***

Caleb was in a slightly better frame of mind when he arrived home late in the afternoon. The tents were not quite the quality the previous rental company was, but they were close enough. He also had the correct measurements so they could order the lights and large-screen TVs and folding chairs. Tim Bennett always stored the stage and podium in his barn so he could pass the numbers along and make sure no modifications would be needed for those items.

His brain was busy listing things that he would need to hand off in the next few days when he stepped in his house. The warm smell of roast beef hash wafted toward him. After putting his briefcase in his study, he headed to the kitchen.

Dawna was just placing bowls of salad next to the two place settings on the kitchen island when he strode in. Her eyes flicked over him before she turned back to the stove without any other acknowledgment of his presence.

A swift feeling of unease rolled through Caleb as he momentarily sensed something was slightly off. He shrugged it away and launched into a discourse on his trip to the Valley and the tents. Dawna remained silent as she pulled a trivet out of the drawer and set the steaming pan of hash on it. Circling the far side of the island, she slid into her chair and folded her hands over her plate. Caleb gave the blessing. The only one talking through the meal was Caleb; the words were meaningless sounds in Dawna's ears.

Chapter Fifteen

"Have a seat. I'll make us some tea," Felicity said as she headed through the small living room in the direction of the kitchen.

Dawna nervously circled around the loveseat to sit. She distracted herself from the question rippling through her mind about why she was here again by looking around.

The room was simple. A loveseat, two chairs, one with a footstool, a slab of log serving as a coffee table, two baskets. The larger one held throws while yarn and knitting needles poked out of the smaller one. Under the windows, a low bookcase reached across the span of the room. Dawna could easily see the titles from her place on the couch. A large number of the books were related to food and cooking; unsurprising given Felicity's business. The rest seemed to be related to what appeared to be feminine studies of various kinds. The top of the bookcase held a collection of female figures. They looked like they were representative of something rather than just decorative, but what she couldn't decipher. Scattered among them were crystals and several small bowls containing organic matter that she guessed was potpourri. The green smell of the land drifted through two partially ajar casement windows.

The room felt safe and she was surprised to find her shoulders dropping slowly. That startled her. Did she walk around with her shoulders pulled up to her ears all the time?

Felicity returned with a tray. She sat it on log table and poured the steaming tea into the two mugs, handing one to Dawna, before moving around to sit on the opposite corner from Dawna. She neither spoke nor questioned, simply waited, holding space for the woman whose face reflected a cascade of changing emotions.

Dawna sipped her tea, mentally starting and discarding ways to explain her presence in Felicity's cabin.

"I'm so lost," she blurted out as she sat her mug back on the table. "I feel like everything I believed and trusted has just been a terrible sham. I don't know why I'm feeling this way or what to do about it." Abruptly, tears started to flow. Felicity got up and disappeared into the kitchen to return bearing a tissue box which she sat between them.

"You have touched the feminine wound that is in the center of all women," Felicity said quietly.

Dabbing at her eyes, Dawna's expression was of pained puzzlement. "I don't understand,"

"It is the place of devaluation that has occurred for many, many millennia where women have been culturally assigned to second-class citizenship in the human race and the border between the two sexes has been land-mined and patrolled by males intent on holding their position of perceived superiority."

Dawna stared out the window as she attempted to process Felicity's words. Did she really feel like a second-class citizen? Wasn't it her role to be submissive to her husband like the Bible said? Didn't it also say that men were to be the head of both families and by extension the church? Why had it become so hard for her to continue in the place she had been assigned? As the questions flowed through her mind, she felt the pool of anger growing within her. Why was the comfortable becoming so increasingly uncomfortable?

Felicity leaned forward. "Dawna, all women feel the wound in their lives. Some are able to brush by it, locking its small nagging pain in a closet, while continuing their socially acceptable roles. Some cannot lock out the pain and they begin to search for the answers.

"Jan was one of those women. For some decades, she filled the roles demanded of her by her CPA husband and her two sons. The day after watching her youngest son graduate from college, she got her first tattoo. It was a small one of a bird rising from an empty nest. She had sketched it thinking it was just her feelings for having completed the hands-on portion of her parenting role. A small private celebration of personal achievement. Her husband flipped his lid and ordered her to laser it off before heading off in a huff to attend some convention.

"She said she sat for two days on the couch and realized that everything that filled her soul was something he denigrated…her art making, the clothes she preferred to the suburban uniforms he required, her personal dreams for her life. In the end, she lasered him out of her life.

"Ophelia and Becca met her at a women's retreat on the coast. She was selling her handmade clothes and jewelry. Ophelia said she knew the minute they met that Jan would be the right person for the vacant space we had here. Lucky for us, she felt the same and joined us here in Summerland."

"Summerland?"

"Yes, it's what we call this place. It has a better ring than Hag Hallow."

Dawna had the grace to blush. "The town's been pretty rotten to you over the years, haven't they?"

"They give us their business, which is enough. We don't need their acceptance or approval."

Dawna studied Felicity's face and knew the woman was speaking her truth.

"How do you do that? How do you not care what other people think about you?"

"Because we've already spent much time examining our own selves, who we are, and aligning ourselves with who we want to be. I guess you can say that we have finally become comfortable in our own skins."

As Dawna looked into Felicity's eyes, the briefest feeling ran through her. It carried the scent of deep peace. It was gone before she could catch hold of it.

Felicity sat her mug down and leaned forward.

"Dawna, living a spiritual life is not a 'one size fits all' proposition. Just as our personhood is completely individual and separate from others, so must our faith be. We must find that which we can slip into tailored for the totality of who we are—our hearts, minds, experiences, personal history. It must heal and strengthen us; serve as both our personal beacon and guide. To find what you need and want, you must be willing to step out of the glare of the patriarchal sun that seeks to blind us to the path found only in the moonlight of our female souls. The sacred illumination in that place can only be gathered in by women. Men seek to keep it hidden because they fear it contains a power they cannot hold or control."

Felicity's words caught in Dawna's chest. They were alien to the millions of words that had been poured in her ears through the decades, but there was also a deep sense of recognition, as though Felicity had triggered some long-forgotten memory within her. She strained to pull it into the light of her thoughts, but it hovered just beyond reach in the liminality of her conscious and unconscious. Abruptly, she shied away as a sense of deep danger passed through her.

"What you're talking about feels wrong," she said.

"Wrong or scary?"

Dawna considered for a moment. "I guess scary is maybe more accurate. It doesn't feel safe."

"No, it's not safe. But then, as women, we are never safe anyway."

Chapter Sixteen

Although she had vowed to avoid Hag Hallow, Mona's craving for one of the deli's chicken salad sandwiches along with a side of the Felicitation potato salad had her turning into the parking lot on her way home from her duties at the church. As she pulled up to the railroad tie, she thought she recognized a parked car. Only when she was getting out did she connect the vehicle to the owner. Mrs. Barnwell must be here picking up dinner for the pastor.

Mona was surprised to see the deli was empty except for a woman who was not Felicity behind the counter.

The woman seemed to know her though. "Hi, Mona. What can I do for you?"

"You're not Felicity," Mona blurted.

"No, I'm Jan. I have the shop next door. Felicity had an appointment so I'm filling in. Don't worry, I have my food handler's card."

A prickle ran up Mona's spine. "How come you know me?"

The woman laughed. "Totem is a very small town. It's not hard to pretty much know who most everyone is. So what can I get for you?"

Mona placed her order and then, backing up several feet, kept a careful eye on the woman with silver-grey dreadlocks pulled back into a bundle as she prepared the sandwich and scooped potato salad into a to-go container.

Slipping the food into a white paper bag, the woman added napkins and a fork before setting on the counter next to the cash register.

Avoiding getting any closer than necessary, Mona held out a twenty-dollar bill as the woman rang up her order and then handed back her change. Mona slipped it into the pocket of her smock. Once she got home, she would put it between the pages of her Bible to cleanse it of whatever evil may have attached. Grabbing the bag, she turned quickly without any further comment and headed to the door. She was unsettled by someone other than Felicity serving her and that added to the sense of sinfulness she felt for even allowing herself to be in Hag Hallow. She wanted to be out of this space as quickly as possible.

Settling her bulk behind the steering wheel, she swung her purse and take-out bag over into the passenger seat before pulling her keys out of her smock pocket, scattering the change she had been given onto the floorboards. Grabbing for the bills, she tossed them beside the bag, leaving the coins to be picked up when she was safely at her house.

As she backed the car up, she caught sight of two women stepping down the gravel tiers from someplace hidden by the storefronts. Shifting the car into drive, she stared at them in her rearview mirror. Yes, one of them was Felicity and the other was—her breath caught as she realized the woman who was now hugging Felicity was the pastor's wife. She had completely forgotten about the unoccupied car she had parked next to. They separated with Mrs. Barnwell, several books tucked under her arm, now heading in the direction of her car while Felicity climbed the stairs to the walkway leading to the deli.

Back at her house, Mona didn't even notice the tastes she had craved all day as she mindlessly stuffed the food in her mouth and chewed. The brief image of the two women embracing looped endlessly in her mind. Mona was confused. She remembered each summer she helped with trying to hand out pamphlets to a bunch of women who showed up for some kind of big weekend thing put on at Hag Hallow. Pastor Barnwell always organized the women to try to save the souls of those who attended. It didn't usually go very well. Most of the people who pulled into the parking lot or parked along the edge of the road just smiled and waved off their offering. A few were a bit nasty about their efforts. It didn't make sense that his wife was now acting all friendly with Felicity.

A memory trickled into her head. Mrs. Barnwell had said at the last women's group meeting she was going to ask the Hag Hallow women to help figure out how the group could better serve the community. Maybe that was what her being there was all about. But why hug? Mona closed her eyes and scrunched up her face as tried to remember if she had ever seen Mrs. Barnwell hug anyone before. Other than a few of the kids from the church, she couldn't remember any other time. She didn't even hug Pastor Barnwell that Mona had ever seen.

Mona sensed an undercurrent of change was putting everything she relied on in her life under some kind of threat. It unsettled her. The unsettling began to spread over into resentfulness. Even though she couldn't figure out exactly why strange things were starting to happen, she felt sure those women were the cause. She would just have to figure out how to make them stop.

Dawna was relieved Caleb was not yet home when she pulled into the driveway. A glance at her dashboard clock indicated there wasn't much time before he would be pulling in. Scooping up the volumes Felicity had given her along with her purse, she hurriedly let herself into the house, making a dash for the office area tucked in the corner of her bedroom to hide the books away. In a flurry, she rushed around, turning on lights and starting dinner. She had already figured out she had the ingredients to throw together spaghetti.

She was breathless by the time she had pans of water and jarred spaghetti sauce with prepackaged meatballs heating. She turned on the oven for the garlic bread and then swiftly set the kitchen island. Only when she was standing the pasta in the boiling water, gently pushing it down as it softened, did she reflect on her actions. They were those of someone who was terrified of being caught doing something wrong and trying to hide it.

Trying to think through why she felt that way, her thoughts looped and tangled as she automatically prepared a salad and put the garlic bread into the oven until a snarled mess lay in the center of her mind. She was so intent on her interior world she actually jumped when Caleb called out that he was home.

Thousands of days of practice allowed her to sweep her own thoughts into a corner called 'later' and apply the majority of her attention to finishing and serving dinner.

As was his habit, Caleb went directly to his study as soon as he had finished eating, leaving the cleanup to her. Operating on a well-honed autopilot, she cleared and cleaned before heading to her own room.

Her first thought was to disguise the books Felicity had loaned her. She went to the bookcase beside her small desk and scanned the shelves for a couple of books encased in dust covers. Stripping them off, she fished the books out from under the recliner where she had hastily stuffed them. Carrying them to her desk, she hid their real subject matter under the cover of something more innocuous.

Satisfied no one would be able to tell their true contents, she sat them carefully on the TV tray she used as a side table before sitting. When she had left Felicity's, she had been so eager to throw herself into the information between their covers. Now, she nervously side-eyed them.

She shifted her gaze to stare out the window at the evening light of the Oregon summer. They had passed the longest day of the year. She always loved the long, light evenings of summer and felt a pang once the solstice was behind them as a few minutes of the light would disappear each day. She realized it was a mirror for her life. The light she thought she had been living in had disappeared in the same small increments, and now an impending winter seemed to be at hand.

Felicity had said a woman's spiritual path lay in the moonlight. Moonlight was only visible in the dark. The concept bothered her. She didn't want to live in the dark. Lowering her eyes to the camouflaged books once more, she suddenly became aware of how much of her life was lived in the darkness of subterfuge; hiding all those parts of herself hungering for things others had told her were unworthy. The TV shows she watched when Caleb was at meetings; the fantasy books she stealthily ordered for her ebook reader; the color books and colored pencils she kept hidden in the back of her desk drawer; the times she stole away to the old cemetery for moments she felt free to think her own thoughts.

It was like she was two people trying to navigate one life. But which was the sinner or the saint?

Chapter Seventeen

Although he frequently disappeared back to his cabin to rest, Trey had taken to tagging along with Evan on some of his various duties. Today he sat on a stump as Evan opened the storage building behind the gazebo. Neatly stacked along the sides and the back were benches. The women were organizing some kind of event that was apparently going to bring in many more than the twenty to thirty women who usually showed up for their weekend workshops. The plan was to shift the tables to the edge of the large area in front of the gazebo and fill it with the benches Evan was now pulling out of the shed.

"So what are you supposed to do with those?" Trey asked as he hunched over his coffee mug.

"Check them and make sure there is no damage and that they're solid. Becca indicated some of their attendees were a bit stout. Then give them a good cleaning so all that had to be done was a dusting when they were set up."

"If they are gonna need all those seats, it must be some big deal they got in the works."

Evan shrugged as he tested the flipped-over bench's supports. He righted it before carrying it to one side.

"Don't know. I set up, I take down, and make myself invisible when they tell me to."

"It doesn't bother you to be ordered around by the women?"

Evan paused for a moment before shaking his head. "Nope. I had plenty of years of running the show. Obviously wasn't as good at it as I thought. I'm okay with leaving that part to them."

He went to pull another bench out of the shed. "It sounds like this is their grand hurrah of the year. Felicity said there would be just a couple more events before they essentially shut down for the winter."

"So what are you going to do then?"

"Still not sure. Can't seem to get the future in focus." He tested the supports on another bench. "Maybe I need to go get advice from Grandfather Tree like Becca suggested, after all."

"Grandfather Tree? He's still standing?"

Evan shot a look of surprise at Trey. "You know about it?"

"Sure. It was another of Eleanora's things. She was real protective of it. I think she even put some kind of spell or something around it."

Skepticism was clear in Evan's voice. "A spell?"

"Yeah. I know this is going to sound real far-fetched but it's the gospel truth, I swear. I told you about the old cabin that used to be up where Ophelia's gardens are, right?"

Evan nodded as he upended another bench.

"Well, me and Duane was up there partying like usual and Duane got this idea that we should carve our initials into Grandfather Tree. It was dumb-ass, but we were flying high so it seemed like a good idea at the time. Anyway, we went stumbling off into the woods with this big old Bowie knife Duane always carried to do the deed. Duane figured he oughta go first since it was his knife. So when we finally found it, Duane goes charging in ready to start hacking at the bark." Trey stopped as he began to try to draw is some deep breaths.

Evan stopped. "You okay?"

Trey took a swig of coffee. "Getting there."

Evan kept an eye on Trey until the man straightened up, rotated his shoulders a few times before once again hunching over. "So where was I?"

"Duane charging the tree."

"Okay, yeah. Me, I was right with him. Anyway, as soon as we got within like about three feet of that tree, it was like we ran into something. Now, this was summer and the air was pretty warm even at night, but suddenly it turned as cold as midnight in January. And it was like there was something in that air. Something dangerous. I was the most scared I've ever been in my life. Duane too. We hightailed it back to the cabin and never went near it again."

Evan thought about the number of times he passed Grandfather Tree; even, occasionally, stopping to give it a gentle pat. He felt a deep respect for something that had lived through and seen as much history as that great old Douglas fir had. "I've never felt anything when I've been around it."

Trey shrugged. "Eleanora's gone. Maybe her spells and stuff went with her."

"And maybe I never thought to take a knife to him."

Trey nodded. "Yup, there's that."

Silence stretched across the warming morning air before Trey broke it. "I'd like to ask a favor. I was wondering if I might borrow your van for any hour or two one day. Don't quite trust myself with the bike anymore. There's one more thing I need to square away here in Totem."

Evan leaned back on his haunches. "Sure. Tell me when and I'll get you the keys. Wouldn't be a problem driving you, either, if you'd prefer."

Trey ducked his head. "'Preciate that, but it's kinda personal. Something I've been running from for fifty years. I, at least, owe him some explanation."

When Evan glanced at Trey, he thought he saw the silhouette of a man standing behind him. He started to say something when Trey shifted slightly on the stump. The image disappeared. Just a shadow from the trees.

Chapter Eighteen

Jan was down on her hands and knees in front of her store's door with a whisk broom the next morning when Evan climbed the steps heading to the deli. He paused and watched as she shoved a line of white stuff into a pile before directing it into a dustpan.

"Everything okay?" he asked.

She looked up at him with a disgruntled twist to her mouth. "Salt in front of the doors... again."

Lack of understanding was obvious in Evan's face. "Salt?"

Standing up, Jan stepped down a couple of the stairs before flinging the contents of the dustpan into the gravel. "Yeah. A hoary old purported protection from witches. It's been quite a while since somebody tried it so we must have a new member of our fan club."

"Isn't that a little far-fetched in the 21st century?"

"The branding of primarily women as witches extends back to ancient times. Although it has lost a lot of its potency through the millennia, it has never vanished entirely."

Ophelia emerged from her shop with a cobweb broom and a vintage metal dustpan to gather up the salt strewn in front of her door. She, too, made a wry face at Evan as she carried the dustpan to the stairs and tossed it. A small whirlwind rose and caught the crystals, spinning them up into the air before exploding them over the gravel driveway.

Ophelia shook her head. "Geez, give it a break, Mom," before turning and disappearing back through her door.

Evan looked confused. "Isn't Ophelia's mother dead?"

Jan snapped the handle of the dustpan onto her broom. "She is. It's just that apparently she can't resist phoning in every once in a while. You ought to hear them squabbling on some of those occasions."

She caught the skepticism flashing across Evan's face. "Don't tell me that you've been here, what, seven or eight weeks, and you haven't noticed something that feels different now and again?"

"Yes, actually. Nothing really far-out; just a little inexplicable."

"Well, don't be surprised if the far-out jumps up one of these days," Jan grinned as she headed to her shop door.

Evan turned towards the deli. Jan's remark had unsettled him. Most everything he had labeled 'inexplicable' was minor stuff he shrugged off. Should he be paying more attention, and if so, to what?

Since Felicity opened the deli earlier than the other businesses, any trace of the salting incident that might have occurred in front of her door was gone when Evan pushed through.

Lifting her eyes only a moment from the bagels she was slathering with cream cheese, she nodded in the direction of a carafe and a couple of mugs sitting on the end of the counter. "It's a help-yourself morning," she said. "Got maple brown sugar oatmeal that should be done in just a few."

"Anything I can do to help?" Evan asked as he crossed to the coffee.

"Thanks, but I'm almost done. Library is having some kind of meeting this morning and decided at eight o'clock last night they maybe should provide refreshments." She arranged the bagels on a paper platter, then deftly pulled out a length of plastic wrap from an industrial roll to cover them with.

"That's a bit after hours," Evan noted.

Setting the platter on top of an already loaded box, Felicity grinned as she started to clean up. "You know, that is the one thing about itsy bitsy towns. People really don't have any concept that some places in the world really do operate only during designated hours. Here, they know you, they call you."

The door opened and a woman bustled in looking every inch a small-town librarian from her wire-rimmed glasses to her sensible foam-soled shoes.

Evan politely headed to his usual spot as the woman breathlessly thanked Felicity, grabbed the box, stopping only long enough to explain the need to send the bill to city hall for payment before rushing out the door again.

As soon as the door closed, Felicity answered the disappearing woman, "Right, Lucille, we've only been doing this over twenty years. I think I have the drill down."

Evan was tucking into the bowl of oatmeal when Felicity dropped into the chair opposite him, taking a long sip from her coffee cup.

"So did you have salt as well?" Evan asked between bites.

"Yup. Leave no door unseasoned has always been the motto."

Evan leaned back after spooning up the last bites of oatmeal and reached for his own coffee cup. "Where does all this witch stuff come from anyway?"

"Mostly just third-hand gossip, usually from those that were here when Eleanora was still alive."

"Trey told me a few things about her. He seems convinced she was a witch, complete with spells and everything."

"Trey would. They were constantly at loggerheads. If Eleanora said he needed to go right, he would damn well head left every time."

"This is going to sound strange, but Ophelia seemed to think her mom was here this morning."

Felicity gave him an odd look. "She did? Interesting." She turned her head and looked out the window. "And what is that boding?"

An uncomfortable feeling passed through Evan. Maybe Jan was right. Maybe things were a little weirder here than he had been willing to acknowledge. He shifted uneasily in his chair.

Felicity looked back at him. "Eleanora is our early-warning system. When she starts drifting around, something has gone into motion that will affect Summerland sooner or later. It totally aggravates Ophelia, who likes to think of herself as our own personal prophetess, usually of doom, when her mother shows up."

Okay, things just moved a lot closer to the far-out side than he was sure he knew how to handle.

It must have shown in his face as Felicity suddenly flashed him a grin. "I'm sorry, Evan. You must feel like you inadvertently stepped into some badly written gothic novel. Witches, ghosts, and broken-down old men telling tall tales of past spookiness. I will be glad to fill you in with some details about why all this strangeness, but I'm not sure it will assuage your perception of us."

Evan got up and headed to grab the coffee carafe on the end of the counter. Returning, he refilled both their cups before sitting back down. He looked expectantly at Felicity.

"Eleanora Swanner was a true force of nature. She had remarkable gifts that definitely would have gotten her burned at the stake in another time.

"She read people like they were carrying neon signs announcing their situation. She always knew who had a desperate need of any kind and she had no compunction about wading in to help whether it was providing her medicinals, food, or extricating some living thing from an abusive environment."

"Trey mentioned she apparently told people things," Evan said.

Felicity laughed. "Oh, she was notorious for that. She'd corner the towns-people all the time to whisper something in their ear. Although she never revealed what she told someone, she must have hit the nail on the head more often than not because everyone got shaky when they saw her coming."

"I can see where people might get the idea she was a witch."

"She definitely had her own magic. She was incredibly plugged into the universe and had the courage to act on whatever it was telling her at the time. And you are right. People did come to believe she was some kind of witch and she had no problem embracing that image if it suited her purpose."

"And how does that apply to the four of you?"

"Besides Jan, who is relatively recent, we're her offspring. Well, Ophelia is her offspring, but she wrapped Becca and myself into her life when we were young so many assume the fruit does not fall from the tree."

Evan abruptly sniffed a couple of times, turning his head and looking around. "Do you smell smoke?"

Felicity drew in a deep breath. "Yup. It's cigarette smoke."

Looking out the window, Evan looked up and down the walkway in front of the deli. "Nobody's out there."

"Ophelia's right. Eleanora's here. She smoked liked a chimney. So I guess we're in for it—whatever it may be."

Chapter Nineteen

Pam was just clearing off her desk when Dawna entered balancing two mugs of hot water in one hand and carrying a white bag in the other. She sat them on the desk as Pam picked up a plant with striped leaves, carrying it carefully to the window and setting it in the sill.

"Hey that's beautiful and new," Dawna remarked.

"Ophelia gave it to me last week when I stopped by to pick up Mom's foot lotion."

Dawna opened the bag she was carrying. She pulled out a breakfast sandwich to sit beside the mug she had placed in front of Pam's chair before retrieving her own. "Something to get us through folding the revival programs." Turning the bag on end, she shook out two teabags.

"Honey vanilla?"

"Honey vanilla," Dawna confirmed. "So what is it?" She nodded towards the plant as she unwrapped her sandwich.

"Something that is perfect for a church secretary's office. It's a prayer plant. Supposedly it folds its leaves up like in prayer when it gets dark. I haven't seen if that was true yet since it's always light when I head home."

Dawna eyed it thoughtfully. "Never heard of it."

"Me neither until it was presented to me."

"So how is it going and how is your mom doing?"

"Better. The infusions are definitely stabilizing her. She's eating and sleeping well and she's just perkier; more herself. And, with the lotion from the Green Apothecary, her peripheral neuropathy stays quiet enough she can move around comfortably."

"It's all herbal stuff, right?"

"Yup. Ophelia raises the plants she makes her concoctions from, just like her mother did. I'm guessing a lot of her formulas were passed down to her by Eleanora, and judging by Mom's situation, I will say they work pretty darn well."

"Wasn't that the lady Bethany mentioned at the last women's group meeting?"

Pam nodded as she chewed the bite of sandwich she had taken. "Eleanora was…" she paused before concluding, "unique."

"How so?"

"Well, you heard Bethany's story. It was one of many, many similar happenings. On one hand, she was adored for her constant acts of kindness by some of the townspeople, and on the other, she could rile up some people to the point of them threatening to burn her house down with her in it. The town had a real love/hate relationship with her. In fact, when she died, not a single church in the town would conduct the funeral. Alan and Bethany paid to lay her to rest."

"Not even Caleb?"

Pam gave her a strange look. "Especially Caleb."

"Why especially?"

"I'm not sure; all I know is he came storming in one day absolutely spitting bullets about her. Never said why, other than to say she was never to be mentioned again in his hearing."

"When was that?"

"Sometime shortly after he took over pastoring the church. I don't think it was long before she passed. He never said anything to you?"

Dawna shook her head. "No, never."

There was a noise in the hallway and when both women looked towards the door, they saw Mona standing there clutching her cleaning tote. She pointed to the Pam's desk. "The deli was open today?"

Dawna looked puzzled. "Of course. If I had known you would have liked something, I would have gotten it for you."

In answer, Mona turned and fled down the hallway toward the sanctuary.

Dawna and Pam exchanged puzzled glances before shrugging. Sometimes there was no figuring out Mona.

***

Caleb fell back in his chair after sending Mona on her way. The day had been one of the worst he had endured for a long time. The revival preparations had turned into nothing but one disaster after another.

The rigging company which always handled the lighting and electrical set-up for the microphones, the TVs, and the sound system had suffered a fire at the business and would not be able to fulfill their normal contract until they could secure some essential new equipment and that was not likely to happen in time to meet the church's timetable. Alan was trying to find another company on very short notice. Then Tom stopped in to let him know the stage frame had dry rot and needed some rebuilding to be safe while simultaneously reminding Caleb it was bean season and, while he would do what he could, Tom had to focus on getting his crops to market. The finish to the day was Mona letting him know Dawna had apparently taken to stopping by to visit Felicity, something that might reflect badly on the church if other people noticed when they were this close to the revival.

His mind began to enumerate the litany of problems dropped on him the past few months. Trey showing up alive, tent companies closing, rigging businesses burning, stages rotting, and even his own wife fraternizing with the Hag Hallow women all felt like personal betrayals. Angrily he flung himself out of his chair and began his methodical shut-down of the church.

Dawna was setting a selection of salad dressings next to a basket of crackers when he entered the kitchen. She pulled two plates of cobb salad out of the refrigerator followed by a pitcher of lemonade.

Caleb mechanically gave the blessing before picking up his fork. Although he said nothing, Dawna could feel the waves of anger coming from him. She guessed they had to do with the various hurriedly called meetings he had with different people today and were most likely connected to the revival. Since he had made it clear her role was relegated to overseeing the food, and the ladies involved, she felt no obligation to offer succor to him.

After eating, he abruptly left the kitchen without saying a word to her. She set about cleaning up and loading the dishwasher. She had just pushed the start button when he reappeared. Leaning against the island, he crossed his arms over his chest.

"So Mona tells me you have been seen talking to Felicity Sewell."

A geyser of anger shot up in her. "I don't recall Mona Weiner has any business in my business," she said through clenched teeth.

"The point is, if Mona saw you talking to Felicity, who knows who else in town saw you. It is not a good image to be showing, especially so close to the revival. It might put people off attending."

"You know, Caleb, those women are not the devil's spawn. They are just old ladies who have made their own life in Totem, and from what I have heard here and there, they have done right by the town for a long time."

"You didn't grow up here. You have no idea about their antecedents. They may well be the devil's spawn."

"Ophelia's mother? People can't help who they're born to."

"Not all of them were born to her. They chose to follow her."

"Follow her? From what I've been able piece together, she took in and cared for a couple of young girls who were left motherless."

"They could have gone to a good Christian home."

"Yes, they could have, except apparently no one offered them one. And why are we fussing over events that happened decades ago?"

Caleb drew a deep breath. "I just want you to stay away from there until after the revival. I've got enough problems with it right now. I don't need any more."

"I won't be staying away because Felicity does part of the food for the Friday night meal," Dawna said with a lift of her chin. "So maybe before you jump down my throat based on something Mona ran to tattle on, you might want to consider I was doing the same thing I have done for years. Meeting with Felicity to figure out the food."

Caleb flushed. He didn't pay a lot of attention to the side of the revival the women handled other than to set the budget. Even though he knew the deli supplied some things for the meals, he had never wondered how they were procured. He turned abruptly and walked out of the kitchen.

Dawna sagged against the sink. That was the first time she had spoken a complete lie to her husband. Although she expected to be swamped with guilt, only a fleeting sense of it passed through her. As she hung the dishcloth over the faucet, she realized that Caleb had not referenced Eleanora directly, instead deflecting to spew his hostility over the Hag Hal…no, wait, what was the name Felicity had used? Summerland. That was it. She decided she would call it the same.

An awareness of how frequently she resorted to derogatory opinions of other people, particularly women, crept into her thoughts as she headed to her bedroom. Instead of sitting down in her chair, she began to pace as her brain teemed with remembrances. She realized how much she echoed Caleb's words. A sense of horror wafted through her. Where in time had she slipped into being just a badly smudged rubberstamp of her husband? When had she given up making her own mind about things?

She sat down. Lord, it dated clear back to when they first moved to Totem. Caleb had grown up here. He knew the town while she knew nothing. To avoid making some kind of mistake that would put him and the church in an awkward light, she had taken to adhering closely to his opinions and actions. It had become such a habit that by the time she had enough knowledge to make her own judgments, she continued to go along.

Her thoughts scampered around. Everything they touched had someone else's fingerprints on it. Only her very recent actions in meeting with Felicity held no outside input or influence. It jolted her.

Now she could interpret what she had felt in Felicity's presence sitting on her loveseat. Felicity unapologetically knew who she was. She owned her thoughts, feelings, life and she gave little credence to the opinions of others.

A huge wave of envy rolled through her. She had lived almost all her life chained to the opinions of others, constantly chipping off pieces of herself to fit their expectations. She had almost eradicated her own soul in seeking the light of others' approval.

Felicity said she would find the answers in the dark where the moonlight was visible. She got that now. She was telling her she needed to search for all the things she had hidden in the shadows within using only the light of herself.

A miasma of concern began to spread through her. What if she journeyed into the darkness only to find nothing left?

***

Far from soothing his concerns, Dawna's perfectly rational explanation about meeting with Felicity fueled the seething frustration Caleb was feeling. Revival was usually his favorite time of the year. He loved standing up in front of the people who came to hear his words. Through the over thirty years he had been doing it, he had honed it into an event that pulled money out of pockets and into the church coffers. It also garnered him a certain amount of personal recognition that translated into speaking engagements at various conferences and retreats. Things he believed he richly deserved given his dedication to his profession. And now it was like everything was conniving to thwart him this year.

It wasn't just the technical aspects falling into disarray. He felt something drifting around the edge of his life he couldn't identify or clarify; an amorphous shadow he caught just outside of his consciousness now and again. It was all throwing him off his stride.

Pushing back against the thoughts churning in his brain, he turned to his computer and tapped the touchpad. Awakening, the screen revealed a blank page with a single line at the top, Loving One Another in the Current Times. He stared at it, his fingers poised above the keys, waiting for words to form. Several minutes passed. Nothing appeared.

When he had chosen this year's theme, he had felt like it was a topic he could have talked on for a week. Now he couldn't seem to find his way to the first sentence. All the original concepts had disappeared. Abruptly, he wished he had chosen another topic, but the programs were printed and the advertising in motion. There was no going back.

He slumped back in his chair before spinning away from his desk to stare at the bookcase behind him. As his eyes drifted around his collection of books looking for something to inspire him, they fell on a small, framed photo in the corner of the third shelf.

That one serrated edged snapshot captured the very first revival he had attended as a boy—the moment that ultimately set the course for his life. He had been invited by his best friend whose family was part of a more evangelical church than his own.

Looking back, he understood how hokey it had really been. Unseen hands had pulled dime-store rubber snakes across the floor of the stage as the evangelist acted out the story of Moses and the bronze snake from the biblical book of Numbers. The execution may have been amateurish but the message of unwavering faith in all things had hit the attendees hard. He witnessed tears and nearly everyone had gone to the stage when the altar call was made at the end. Even he had gone forward with his friend. At the conclusion, he and his friend had taken turns using an old box camera to get pictures of themselves with Preacher Wilbur Snelling, the man with his arm around the shoulders of his own young image.

Fascinated and surprised by the congregants' frequent outbursts of "amen" and "hallelujah, brother" during the services, in contrast to the quiet steadiness of the services at the traditional church his parents attended, he began to tag along with Ben more and more frequently.

By high school, he had decided he truly had been chosen to save the souls of others. He studied the lives of evangelists like Billy Graham, Dwight Moody, the Wesley brothers, and Billy Sunday while daydreaming about his own biography one day inspiring future students.

The vision of leading his own revivals had been on hold for some years while he served as a placeholder pastor until some church selected a permanent candidate. Then, by what he always felt was the hand of God, he was called back to his hometown. Totem had grown, although not substantially, but enough that pitching the first small tent had been most fulfilling.

Through hard work and careful cultivation, his annual soul-saving event now drew hundreds to the small town. He mentally basked in the memories of previous revivals where he could assume full credit for those who came forward to claim their salvation.

A shadow passed over his thoughts and then her voice was in his head. "Doesn't matter how many souls you think you are saving, Caleb. It's the one you didn't that will matter."

Chapter Twenty

Mona had done a stealth drive-by of Hag Hallow in the break between her cleaning and the women's meeting. There were several cars in the parking lot. The woman who owned the Green Apothecary was standing in her open door chatting with someone on the wooden porch. Another person was just leaving the deli with a white bag in hand. Everyone seemed to be operating as they did every day.

Driving back to the church, she struggled to understand what went wrong. Miss Kepler had been so sure that salt deterred witches.

Pam was setting carafes of coffee and hot water for tea on the table when Mona entered the fellowship hall. Taking her place at the table, Mona didn't see the usual agenda in front of her chair. In fact, the only things on the table were the other women's notepads.

She felt a stirring of agitation. The agenda was always part of the meeting. "I didn't get an agenda," she said.

Pam nodded. "Dawna is bringing the agenda with her. She should be here any minute."

Watching Dawna closely as she strode into the room, Mona failed to interpret the hard look Dawna shot at her before setting the papers she carried on the table and pulling out her chair. Bethany poured hot water into one of the mugs and shoved the bowl with envelopes of tea towards Dawna.

Dawna poked through the bowl before pulling out one. When she dropped the freed teabag in her cup, a waft of cinnamon rose in the steam.

"So did you have a chance to talk with Felicity?" Bethany asked.

"I did."

"Did she give you some ideas on how we can start an outreach program?"

Dawna nodded as she swirled the teabag in her mug. "Yes and no." She pulled the bag out, setting it on its envelope. "What she gave me made me start thinking about our role as women here in the church. It occurred to me we might need to examine ourselves to find out who we are or might be in order to have something to take out into the larger community."

Nan looked puzzled. "Okay," she said slowly, confusion evident in her voice.

Dawna leaned forward over the table. "Basically, we are just adjuncts at this point. Everything we do and are allowed to do is just to support the men's vision. What is our vision as women? What do we really want to do as opposed to what we are allowed to do?'

"Do I sense a rebellion in the making?" Pam asked.

"Maybe more of a way to claim our own space at the Lord 's Table in order to make meaningful contributions beyond the 'kitchen and nursery' as Trish pointed out."

Bethany nodded. "I think I'm getting your drift. At home and in our business, Alan treats me as a complete equal. He never makes a decision without inviting my input and respecting what I offer. It's only here that I feel I need to stand behind him and keep my mouth shut."

"That's pretty much the same way I feel. We are to be seen but not really heard from." Nan added.

"It really came home to me at the last revival," Pam said thoughtfully. "We work our butts off doing all the food and clean up, and then we are shuffled to the back of the overflow tent like outside hired help instead of appreciated full members here. I would never have allowed Hank to do that to me when he was alive. Why do I let myself be treated that way here?"

"Then you would not be opposed to starting a women's ministry here?" Dawna asked.

Silence hovered above the table as the women contemplated the concept.

"I guess it would depend on who would lead it," Bethany said. "I feel like it would have to get really personal to be effective and I'm not really comfortable with someone I didn't know well coming in."

"I would lead it," Dawna said.

She caught the slightly startled looks the women exchanged. "I don't think it was ever really put out here when we first came, but Caleb and I met in Bible College. I graduated with the same degree, a Bachelor's in Bible Studies, as Caleb. In fact, I was valedictorian of our class and, during the time we were moving around while he took on temporary pastoral duties, I got my Master of Theology."

"Wow, that has been a well-kept secret," Pam exclaimed, her mouth hanging open.

"It was something we agreed to when he accepted the position here. He wanted time to establish himself without fear of, perhaps, confusing the congregation. When he felt secure in his pastoring, we were supposed to gradually build a joint ministry. Needless to say, that has never happened."

"But only men are supposed to be pastors," Mona blurted. "The Bible says so."

Dawna looked at her patiently. "Women have ministered and advised each other through traditional means such as circles for many millennia now, including Biblical times. The women of Summerland are a fine example of that."

"Summerland?" Nan raised her eyebrows in question.

"That is the name the women gave to the property they own," Bethany answered. "Hag Hallow is what many call it to diminish their connection with the town."

"But women can't save people's souls," Mona answered. "Only Pastor Barnwell can do that."

"You know, Mona, Caleb can't save every soul either. Sometimes they save themselves," Dawna answered.

Chapter Twenty-One

Evan sat on the stoop of his cabin, twisting the top off a chilled beer. The late July day had been a hot one, causing Trey to beg off their evening ritual of sharing cold brews and conversation after dinner.

While it was tempting to just hole up in the air-conditioning of the cabin, Evan had come to love watching the shadows of the fir trees creep across the land as the sun set behind them until they melded into the dusk. He wondered at himself for spending so many decades being so strictly focused on the expensive watch he wore on his wrist that the outside world was just a blur as he sped through his days. He had crawled on the hamster wheel of 'success', running as fast as he could until the centrifugal force had thrown him out into a place of 'failure'.

It was from that place he had inadvertently found this place. Although initially grateful for the women hiring him and giving him a bunk, he had actually been silently restive the first few weeks as he felt the work was beneath him. He viewed the job simply as a means of acquiring much-needed cash to move on. But oddly his days of dragging wheelbarrows of bark dust around or pulling a rake through the gravel paths and neatening their edges had slowly burned off the anger at the curve life had thrown him. When he fell into bed, he no longer tossed and turned carrying on mental conversations of retaliation and self-justification as physical weariness brought almost instant sleep.

As time passed, he lost the beat of his former life. Other things began to creep into his consciousness. The first light of day touching the tops of the trees and gradually washing down until the world was illuminated; the rustle of small creatures in the woods; the occasional call of a coyote hidden high on the ridge; the ever-changing flora and fauna.

Watching the shadows cross the pond on their way to the highway running alongside the eastern edge of the property, he again pondered the whole odd way he came to be sitting on these steps and what might have happened to him if the women hadn't dragged him out of his van and into their lives.

From various bits of information, he had been given over the course of his time here, he knew Becca's brothers had signed over their portions following their dad's death, apparently anxious to be permanently shut of Totem. Somehow Becca managed to keep the old store running and hang onto the land despite pressure from some to sell. When Ophelia's mother passed, Ophelia sold her farm, and she and Felicity joined Becca in rebirthing the old Calhoun property. He wasn't sure how many decades of work they had put in before it came to be the place he was now familiar with.

It was difficult for him to reconcile the stories Trey told him of the property's crude past with the serenity it now held; almost a sense of otherness, as though some invisible aspect kept the ugliness of the rest of the world from spilling in. Maybe the strange little figurines really did work, he thought, remembering the tiny one he found tucked into the knothole of a tree. Periodically, he would spot others in odd locations. When he mentioned it to Becca, she just smiled and said, "Never hurts to have a little extra protection in these parts."

Considering some of the women's eccentricities, he could see why some in the community might label them witches. Ophelia planted the vegetable crops based on the phases of the moon and even insisted that root crops be planted at night in the light of the full moon. She harvested by touching the plants, particularly in her medicinal beds, to determine whether they were ready. Two plants might look identical in size and foliage to him but after running her fingers over the plant, she would take one and leave another as not being ready for reasons he could not discern.

Jan had a whole litany of ways she cleansed the crystals she used in her jewelry making. Some she left sitting in the sun. Others only saw the light of the moon, and a few got buried in Ophelia's herb beds. He once saw Jan with a large package of beads she had ordered. Knowing she only used handmade beads from various artisans, he was surprised to see her sitting on the steps outside her store methodically smashing a pile back to clay dust. Assuming they had sent her the wrong item, he asked why she didn't just return them. She shook her head at him. "No, these just need to go. Bad juju" she said, crushing another with a flat stone.

He had learned not to be startled when he saw stinging nettle or young fiddlehead ferns included in meals. Becca foraged with the help of Enoch, Felicity cooked, and it was all delicious.

He had no idea if the women threw anything mystical into their workshops, but they appeared pretty innocuous as far he could see. Becca's wild crafting and foraging, Jan's mandala and personal jewelry making, Ophelia's herbal-related classes all seemed to be mainstream New Age, although he had to admit some of the attendees he occasionally spotted, looked like they might know how to stir up a spell or two.

Now some kind of big three-day feminine-focused event was planned for the latter part of August. Felicity had given him a heads-up that it was going to get a bit frenetic for the next few weeks. Boxes were beginning to loom large in his days as he had picked up materials at the printers. Totes of fairy lights, battery-run candles, and other things were hauled down to the storage shed behind the gazebo for future set-up while plans were drawn up of where to place tables that would be brought up and arranged along the walkway for luncheons during the event.

This increasing burst of activity was marking the end of his agreement with the ladies. The thought of moving on had lost its appeal. During his time here, he reawakened the forgotten pleasure of working with his hands instead of strictly his brain. There was satisfaction in seeing the immediate results of his efforts. Once he understood what they wanted of him, they left him to determine how and when he did particular tasks, not even checking to ensure he had done them.

He had come to genuinely like and respect the ladies. Not once since they pulled him out of the van had they ever attempted to intrude on his personal boundaries, allowing him to determine what he might want to disclose of his past.

Although he knew it was impractical, as the work he provided would dwindle off when winter approached, he found himself wishing he had more time here. He drew in a deep breath and smelled cigarette smoke. It carried an odd perturbation like something was in the offing and he was inextricably bound to it.

Chapter Twenty-Two

Felicity and Dawna were both writing in their respective notebooks as they discussed the food items Felicity would be providing for the revival. Dawna dropped her pencil with a sigh. "If only the men knew how much we hate being relegated to the kitchen. Their souls get all the attention while we don't seem to matter other than making sure they're fed."

"I don't understand," Felicity said, reaching for her tea.

Dawna explained how it worked for the women based on past revivals, ending with them being shunted to the back of the overflow tent.

Felicity's face broke into a wicked smile. "How about the girls and I come and do the serving so you can participate? Wouldn't that get their tighty whiteys in a wad?"

Dawna looked momentarily shocked before giggling. "That would be something, wouldn't it." She fiddled with her pencil for a moment before asking, "What was he like when you were growing up?"

"Who?"

"Caleb. If I'm remembering right, you went to school the same time he did."

"Actually, he was a couple of years ahead of me."

"Was he always so sure of himself and … rigid?"

Felicity scrolled back through her memories. "I can't say that I really paid much attention to him or most of the people who I was in high school with until I was an upper classman, although Totem High School was pretty small back then. My mom was diagnosed with breast cancer the summer before I started my freshman year. Other than actual classes, I spent most of my time helping her with her little bakery and catering business. About the only people I spent much time with were Becca and Ophelia.

"She passed just a few months into my sophomore year. By the time I came out of the fog of losing her, my brother, Trey, and Caleb were graduating, so all I have is some of the things they said about him, and, frankly, I have no idea if any of it was truthful. Duane couldn't handle Mom's situation and was running pretty wild.

"Anyway, according to them, Caleb was a real prig. He apparently was always toting his Bible and, I guess, acting like he was superior to most everyone else. He was also a snitch, constantly turning in kids for smoking behind the school grandstands, cutting class, or getting drunk on the weekends, three of my brother and Trey's favorite things to do."

"He mentioned a Trey that he had gone to school with coming back to town a few months back. He wasn't happy about it."

"I imagine not. My brother and Trey were total hellions and, although I don't know for sure, I'd be willing to bet they did their best to make his life miserable in one way or another, but that was a very long time ago," she said. "Duane has been dead for decades and Trey is a sick old man. Can't imagine why it would matter to him now."

"Maybe it doesn't really. A lot of things seem to be going wrong for the revival this year. Maybe he just needed a place to vent his frustration." Dawna paused. "I'm thinking about starting a women's ministry at the church," she said impulsively.

Felicity smiled at her. "Don't think, do."

"It's not that simple. Caleb will insist he has to get permission from the deacons and that now is not a good time because of the upcoming revival, and, frankly, he will find a hundred excuses to put it off even after revival." There was a bitter note in her voice. "We went through this already. I wanted to have a program for the women during revival since all the meetings are pretty much focused on the men. He made sure it was a no-go."

Felicity pursed her lips thoughtfully before asking, "Would you have to have it at the church or could you do it elsewhere?"

The thought startled Dawna. "We do most things at the church, but some are done elsewhere. Pam does Bible study at her house."

"Then how about doing it here? It would have to be in the evening, of course, but I could leave refreshments and you can arrange the tables any way you want to."

Dawna turned and took a careful look around the compact room. "This might work, but it would depend on how much you would want to charge for us to use it. Caleb is very tight with the church budget."

Shaking her head, Felicity said, "Nothing. Women need a safe place to explore their spirituality and that is one of the tenets of Summerland… offering a safe place when a need arises. I also think it would allow more freedom if you were not enclosed in a structure so steeped in the patriarchy."

For a moment, excitement shone in Dawna's eyes before fading. "Who am I kidding? I'm so lost myself right now, I don't even know what I'd be able to teach or lead with."

"Maybe you don't have to lead or teach. Maybe the questions you are struggling with would apply to them as well."

"I don't understand."

"If I've been interpreting your words correctly, it appears that most of what is presented at the church is directed at the men, correct?"

Dawna nodded.

"Well, isn't it possible that other women might be in the same place as you—wanting to find their way to the center of their feminine faith? I think a safe, open exploration of questions might be the way to go."

"You mean have no preset service?"

"Exactly. You've trod that highway for a long time under Caleb. It might be more useful if you did a little wandering in the wilderness. I'm pretty sure both John the Baptist and Jesus spent time there finding some answers."

Dawna leaned back in her chair, staring out the window. Felicity's words felt right. She wasn't Caleb. She wasn't out to save someone else's soul. She was looking to find her own and maybe some of the answers she needed lay in the hands of others.

"Would it matter what day we could use it?"

"Any day Monday through Friday. We hold workshops on the weekend, so it is trickier because my hours run later. Any time after six p.m. is best."

Dawna looked thoughtful. "Pam usually hosts Bible study on Tuesdays because of services on Wednesday. Maybe we could combine the two. Let me talk to her and get back to you if that's okay?"

"I'm going to take that as a commitment. Not to me, but to yourself, which is as it should be."

The flare of excitement bubbling in Dawna's midsection eroded into a jittery feeling as the distance between the deli and the church shortened. She was relieved when she pulled into the parking lot and Caleb's car was not present. Pam's was the only vehicle. She took that as an auspicious sign given her mission.

Pam was opening the mail when she entered and dropped into the chair in front of her desk.

"Hey, Dawna. Caleb's run off the check on the repairs Tom made to the stage. Not sure when he'll be back."

"Good, because I want to discuss something with you." She outlined her conversation with Felicity. "So what do you think? Should we do it?"

"Let me chew on that for a moment while I get us some tea."

Returning, she set one cup in front of Dawna before circling the desk and sitting down. "I like the idea but I'm not sure how some of the other women, especially our older ladies, would take it."

"Oh, it wouldn't be obligatory for anyone. It would be an open invite. Come if you want, or not. Individual choice."

Pam blew across the surface of her tea before taking a sip. "What kind of service are you thinking of providing."

"No service. We get that here. More of an opportunity to raise questions and seek answers as to who we are as women of faith and how we can best use it to address the needs of the community."

Pam stared over Dawna's shoulder for a moment before looking back at her. "Kinda a break from the church then?"

Dawna shook her head. "No. More of a way of finding our own ground to stand on instead of always being told where to stand."

"I like it. I say let's go for it. I don't mind folding Bible study into it. There's only one issue I can think of."

Dawna raised her eyebrow in question.

"What are we going to do about Mona? Because she is not going to like the change."

"Caleb neither," Dawna answered.

***

"I just don't have time to deal with this idea of yours," Caleb said when Dawna broached it as they finished their dinner.

"There is nothing required of you," Dawna countered. "This would be a women's ministry, by the women for the women."

"And who would lead it, if not me?"

"I would."

"And what makes you think you are qualified to represent the church?"

Dawna stared at Caleb, her jaw hardening. "I think you know the answer to that as well as I do."

Caleb flushed. He tended to not give his wife credit for doing the same work as he had done in preparing to be a minister. In fact, more than he had, as she had continued on for her Master's; something he had encouraged as a way to keep her from taking on a more active role in the churches he served as an itinerant pastor.

"Well, you will have to get the approval of the deacons. You know that's required for instituting any new programs. And, of course, there is no money available to fund it and I'm not sure when you would be able to use the church building as there is something scheduled most nights."

And there it was. Exactly what she had expected would come out of Caleb's mouth: barriers to her plan. She was prepared.

"This will not be a program of the church. It will be independent and open to women of any church or no church. We don't need to use the church. We've been offered a place gratis that would serve admirably, so money is also not required."

His mouth opened and closed several times as he searched for more objections. Finally, he pushed away from the kitchen island, pausing only to say, "Just so you know, you do not have my blessing and I will discuss it with the deacons tonight, so don't get too committed."

When Caleb got home, he didn't say anything to her; just disappeared into his office and later into his bedroom. He was equally silent in the morning. It was a call from Bethany that clued her in to last night's meeting.

"Hey, girl, Alan told me that you're actually going to start the women's ministry. Tell me it's true."

"Yes, it's true, so I'm guessing that Caleb did bring it up at last night's deacon's meeting."

"Yes, he did, along with the recommendation that the deacons disapprove of it."

"So what was their decision?"

"Didn't Caleb tell you? They did approve it! Alan told me that several of the men, including him, stated that their wives had often complained about how little was available for them other than acting as quasi-servants. I am so excited I can hardly wait for today's meeting and you better be ready to give us all the details."

"Yup, I intend to, and speaking of that, I better get some print-outs ready. See you this afternoon."

***

Mona was puzzled by the buzz of conversation as the women waited for Dawna to arrive. They seemed to think something exciting was going to happen. The words 'women's ministry' were bandied around. She didn't understand what that meant. Was Pastor Barnwell going somewhere?

There was a smattering of applause when Dawna rushed into the room. "I can't believe you managed to get this past Caleb," Pam said. "I was sure he would try to block it."

Dawna smiled as she sat down. "Actually, it was the deacons who gave us the green light, according to what Bethany told me."

Bethany nodded. "Yup, it was. What Alan told me was that Caleb recommended against it because it might draw us away from performing our duties here in the church and that was more important.

"I guess Tom hit back kinda hard. Told Caleb if the only purpose for women in this church was to wait on the men hand and foot, he was going to recommend his wife find another church that saw women more as spiritual equals and he might just go with her. And Alan backed him up."

"Whoa," Dawna's eyes widened. "No wonder he was in such a pissy mood this morning."

"I just want you to know that I am really excited about this," Nan said. "I just hope we haven't put it off too long. We're not spring chickens anymore."

"No, we're not. But maybe we're in a better place with so many years under our belts. Our bullshit meters are more finely tuned."

Mona gasped. "That's not a nice word."

"Sometimes the nice word doesn't carry enough weight," Pam pointed out.

"I don't understand. What's going on that Pastor Barnwell doesn't like?" she asked.

"We're starting a women's ministry," Dawna answered. She shoved papers from the small pile in front of her toward the other women. "Like we discussed at the last meeting, we aren't being given a lot of spiritual food the way things are now. It's time we began to feed ourselves."

Nan looked up after glancing over the information. "We aren't going to do it here?" she asked.

Dawna shook her head. "No. I feel like if we were to use the space here, we would behave as though the men are still looking over our shoulders and we would unconsciously censor our thoughts as we have done for decades. We have been offered the use of the Felicitations Deli free of charge for a weekly meeting."

"I tend to agree with why we should meet elsewhere, but the deli is an odd choice, don't you think?" Nan asked.

"No. I think it's a good choice," Bethany replied. "There aren't a lot of meeting places in town. The grange charges for use and Caleb apparently made it very clear last night that there would be no money allotted from the church budget for us after the men approved. The library's meeting room is booked solid every night. I know, I'm on the Board, and it would be really awkward to ask another church to let us have space."

"What about your and Alan's office?"

Bethany shook her head. "We would love to host the group, but it is way too small."

"Someone's home?" Pam suggested. "I've had Bible study at the house for years."

"I don't want to put that on anyone," Dawna said. "Whoever was the hostess would most likely feel compelled to clean and prepare refreshment, plus I want this to be accessible, not just to the women of this church, but any woman who might want to attend eventually."

"I hadn't looked at it that way," Nan said. She gave a small smile. "Given that it would happen on neutral ground, I might even be able to get Trish to come to this."

Mona panicked. "But that place is evil. We can't go there."

The other women rolled their eyes and sighed.

That night Mona lumbered from room to room in her house as she paced out her agitation. Everything she had worried about was happening. She had felt it coming for her from the moment she saw Pastor Barnwell's wife in the parking lot with the lady from the deli. Those witches were poisoning the church women. Pastor Barnwell knew it. He had been against this women's ministry. Why couldn't the others see it? Why were they so eagerly following Mrs. Barnwell into sin?

There must be a way to stop them. She would ask Miss Kepler. She had known about the salt. Maybe she knew other ways. Yes, that's what she would do. She would talk to Miss Kepler after the Wednesday service.

Chapter Twenty-Three

As the summer had progressed, Trey no longer regularly appeared for an early breakfast. Evan didn't know if the man was naturally nocturnal or his condition was leaving him less and less energy so he was surprised when he saw him passing by the window on his way to the door of the deli.

Glancing up as he entered, Felicity left the bacon she was frying to pour him a mug of coffee, sliding it across the counter. He nodded at her before heading towards Evan.

Evan watched the silent exchange that marked their interactions with each other. Although he knew they had been married once and things had ended on a particularly bad note, she treated him as though the decades had solidified her long-ago pain into an impenetrable wall he could no longer breach.

Trey made his way to the table. He was oddly silent himself this morning as he doctored his coffee with cream and sugar before sipping it while staring out the window. Evan gave him space while sipping from his own cup. When Felicity sat two plates on the counter, he got up to bring their breakfast to the table. Setting them down, he did another round-trip to bring the small carafe back to top off their cups.

The food seemed to bring Trey's thoughts back to the deli. "Sure appreciate it if I could borrow your van this morning."

"Not a problem. I'll grab the keys when we finish here."

"Be mighty grateful. Comes a time when you just gotta man up and do what you gotta do. Wrong to keep putting it off," he said enigmatically.

Evan could only nod.

When they were through eating, the men left their breakfast plates on the table. Evan had attempted to assist Felicity by delivering them to the counter once only to see a disappointed confusion on Enoch's face. Unwittingly, he had taken away a part of what the man considered his duties. Now he only cleared up after himself when he knew Enoch was off helping one of the other women.

Back in his cabin, Evan retrieved his keys from the tray on the end table. Looking at them in his hand, he realized, of the numerous ones remaining on the keyring, only two had any purpose. He would never use the others from his now dead past. He paused a moment to work them off and drop them into the waste basket. The cabin and van key was the only ones relevant to his life now.

He may have been imagining it, but when the keys hit the bottom, it felt like another door had sealed shut to a place he no longer felt any desire to return to.

Trey was waiting for him, oddly enough with his guitar case.

Reaching for the keys, Trey thanked him. "Don't know how long I'll be gone. I guess until I get things done that I gotta do."

Evan shrugged. "No problem. I won't need it today."

As Trey pulled out of the parking lot, he determined he would head to the stretch of road leading out of town first. He had to concentrate to find it. Was a time he knew every inch of this territory. Now things had changed. There were houses where there had been none, and all the old gravel roads were paved. About the only thing that was the same was there was not much in the way of traffic. He spotted the side road coming out just before the curve in the main road. It had a name now… Halvorson. Made sense. Halvorsons had been about the only people along the road with the exception of a few shanties scattered here and there. Raised turkeys. He and Duane had loved to rev their bikes when they came down the road, exploding the birds into a frenzy.

He slowed as he headed into the curve before finally steering the van onto the narrow shoulder and stopping. Turning on the emergency blinkers, he eased out of the vehicle. He walked around to the back to stare at the stretch right in front of him.

The bright morning faded into early evening. He could hear the roar of their motorcycles in his ear, feel the heavy vibration in his body as he and Duane spun the gravel out from beneath their tires. They barely noticed the pickup truck nosing out of the side road.

Duane had dropped behind him as they came into the curve, both leaning left to maintain their speed as they drifted through it to the straightaway ahead.

He didn't see it happen. But in those helmetless days, he heard the scream of metal hitting metal. He deaccelerated, heading to the edge of the ditch. A pickup accelerated past him, giving him only a glimpse of its bed as it rounded around the curve and disappeared. He didn't hear Duane behind him anymore.

He just let his bike fall as he raced back. Duane lay in the ditch, his bike thrown up on the other side. Blood spurted from his leg that was bent at an inhuman angle.

He had pulled off his belt and tried to fashion a tourniquet, but there was no bone resistance when he pulled it tight and the blood kept coming. Panicked, he looked around desperately for help. It could have been moments or an eternity when he heard the sound of a car engine heading their direction.

He let go of his belt long enough to stand up and wave frantically at them. They pulled alongside as he dropped back down to grab hold of it. No words were exchanged but the car pulled a u-turn and headed back in the direction of town at a good clip.

The blood had slowed to a dribble by the time the town's lone police car pulled up and behind it the ambulance. Duane had given it all and there was nothing left to sustain his life.

He himself was sobbing and begging his friend to hold on—help was here, when the town's officer, Lindquist, pulled him away.

"Let them work, son," he said. Leading him to the other side of the police car, he gently asked. "Tell me what happened."

Between the sobs choking him, he gave over the miniscule knowledge he had about the truck and hearing the crash. Although the officer had deliberately positioned him away from seeing the ambulance volunteers work, he turned when he heard the gurney being pushed through the gravel. Duane was completely covered in a red blanket. One of the men pushing glanced at him and shook his head. He lost it completely at that moment, howling like a wounded animal.

The day brightened as he came back to the present. It was all there; every moment of that horrible evening except one thing. Everyone had accepted it had all happened so fast he couldn't give them any leads on the pickup that hit Duane. But he knew whose truck it was. He had always known.

Climbing back into the van, he pulled a u-turn and headed back toward town. One more stop.

He pulled his guitar case out after parking in the small cemetery lot. Standing on the edge of it, he tried to orient himself to where Duane's grave was. The best he could remember was it was somewhere in the middle. He headed in hoping the small plaque marking it wasn't too faded from the intervening decades. It had been hard enough to scratch up enough money to give him a simple burial with nothing left over to formally mark the grave. A wilted bouquet lying on a tombstone caught his eye. He squinted at it. The flowers looked kinda like some he had seen in Ophelia's beds when he had accompanied Evan to the gardens.

Arriving at the location, he saw that, at some time, Felicity had given Duane a proper marker. He got down on one knee, setting his instrument case to one side, and ran his fingers over the name carved into the granite.

"Hey, man, it's me. I've come back. Yeah, I'm right here in good old Totem. I know it's been a long time since you've heard from me so I guess we need to talk." Trey eased himself down onto the grass.

"Maybe you already know all this since you're in a different place, but I really screwed up my whole life. I guess I couldn't handle you not being there. Nothing worked anymore. Not me, not Felicity, not nothing. It was like someone turned off the sun.

"Remember how we always talked about doing a road trip? Well, one day I climbed on the old bike and took off just like we had always figured we would, except I got lost looking for something I never found and forgot to come back.

"I got to live a whole lot longer than you, but the clock is ticking now. Yeah, things ain't so good so it won't be long before I'm gonna be riding right off this here planet. I'm hoping maybe you'd be waiting there for me when I show up. Could you manage that, man?"

Sitting down, Trey reached over and undid the bungee cord holding his guitar case closed. Pulling the instrument into his lap, he strummed it a few times before turning a couple of keys, and checking it again.

"So, man, this is for us and the past we had. It isn't as good as electric, but it's the best I can do now." He bent over it as he strummed the intro to the song they had adopted as their personal anthem before losing himself in the lyrics of "Born to be Wild." Awash in old memories, he failed to notice someone crossing to his location.

Felicity had recognized Evan's van when she pulled her car alongside it. Her brow furled as she wondered why Evan would be at the cemetery. She didn't think he would even know where it was.

Then she caught the faint sound of a guitar. That puzzled her, too. Stepping onto the grass, she saw someone sitting and playing in the vicinity of Duane's grave. It clicked together. It wasn't Evan. It was Trey.

After a moment's hesitation, she continued in his direction. He didn't seem to notice her approaching. Closing in on him, she recognized the song. She had heard it blasted out enough when they were all young and breathing. The guys had called it their national anthem. They were the easy riders of Totem. It was oddly prophetic.

Trey had his eyes closed as he strummed and sang. It was obvious he was riding down memories of the past. As she stood watching him with Duane's grave between them, a wash of her own memories from the distant past rose up in her. Incense, the smell of the ever so illegal pot, the taste of cheap wine, the lively nights and the languorous days. She had been Etta to their Butch Cassidy and Sundance Kid. A bubble of outrageous youth that burst, scattering them all forever.

As the final chord died away, Trey opened his eyes and realized she was standing there. He squinted in the morning sun as he looked up at her and before the stir of his memories retreated, he saw a very young face. "God, you are so beautiful, girl," he said.

A very slight smile tugged at Felicity's lips as she bent over and picked up the shriveled flowers on the grave, replacing them with the fresh ones in her hand. "The girl disappeared a long time ago," she replied softly. "Nothing left but an old woman now."

Trey didn't seem to hear her. "Them were some times we had, weren't they."

Felicity lowered herself to the ground. "Yes, they were."

"It was him, you know. Duane was the link that tied us together. When he was gone, it was like the whole thing flew apart. He took something with him that left such a huge hole in me. Maybe that was what I was hunting all those years on the road. Something that would fill that big ole empty spot."

"You two had been getting into trouble together since the first grade. Eleanora said you both were cut out of the same soul cloth."

"Eleanora." The words came out like a breath. "She would have known… should have known what was coming, She coulda told us. She coulda changed everything."

"Would you have listened to her even if she had? No. The Duane and Trey I knew back then would have headed out just to prove her and the universe wrong."

Trey dropped his head. "Yeah, pretty much."

Felicity let the stillness of the cemetery settle over them before speaking. "You know, don't you. You know who it was that hit Duane. You've always known," she said softly.

Trey drew in a deep breath as he raised his eyes to scan the trees and sky above her head. The time was now. Time to come clean. It exploded out of him in a single word. "Yeah."

"Who were you protecting?" There was a faint sharpness to her voice now.

"You."

"Me? Someone killed my brother. How was hiding their identity protecting me?"

Trey carefully removed the guitar from his lap and set it in its case. He sat for a moment with his hands on his knees before rubbing them over his jeans. "Because you needed them so much at that time."

"Who? Who did I need?"

"Ophelia and Becca."

"You're not telling me it was one of them. It couldn't have been. We were all at our place that night, getting food ready to do a cook-out when you and Duane got back from your ride."

"It was Ike Calhoun."

Felicity felt like someone had just solidly punched her in the chest.

"Becca's brother?"

"I didn't actually see him, but it was his pickup."

Felicity's eyes flitted around the cemetery before coming back to Trey. "You believe that?"

"I know that. Hell, Duane and I helped Ike repair it more than once. I knew it like I knew my own bike."

She shook her head. "I don't believe it. Ike wouldn't have left Duane to die in the ditch."

"Maybe he got scared. Maybe he didn't even know exactly what happened. I just know that what I saw was the rear end of Ike Calhoun's truck going by me."

Felicity sat with the information. All those years she had wanted to know the truth of that night and now she desperately wished she didn't. She pushed up from the ground, picking up the dead bouquet with her. "I've got to get back. Jan will be wondering where I'm at." She turned toward the parking lot only to turn back. "Please don't say anything to anyone else about what you just told me."

"I've kept it this long. It's not going anywhere else now."

Chapter Twenty-Four

Mona usually hung on every word that came out of Caleb Barnwell's mouth, watching with the adoring gaze of a besotted fan, but the Wednesday service found her twitching in her place on the pew. His words were more like an indecipherable buzz in her ear as she focused on the back of Miss Kepler's head a couple of rows ahead of her. She was so focused she didn't realize the service had come to an end until people started standing up around her and heading to the main aisle.

Although a few headed directly to their cars after the service, the majority moved in the direction of the fellowship hall for refreshments and visiting. Mona trailed after them.

Securing a glass of lemonade and a couple of cookies, she looked around for the elderly lady. She panicked momentarily when she couldn't find her, but then one of the men shifted position and she saw her tucked up at a table in the corner. Mona beelined in her direction.

Pulling out a chair, she immediately launched into her question. "How do you get rid of witches? Make them go away forever?"

Long years had given Miss Kepler the ability to face nonconforming situations with aplomb, and with Mona, the situation was always nonconforming.

Miss Kepler picked up her styrofoam cup before applying a gentle lesson in manners. "Good evening to you, too, Mona. And how are you, dear?" The heavy-set woman just stared. Mona wasn't built for subtleties.

Miss Kepler shook her head slightly and moved on to answer the question. "I am afraid I haven't kept up on more modern ways to banish witches, but in the very olden days, they tended to burn them at the stake; something that is quite frowned upon now."

"That's it?"

"Much of what was done in the long ago was to prevent those deemed to be witches from invading personal space. The burying of iron in doorways, witch balls hung in windows, and other not always savory practices involving bodily fluids and nails were done to keep the witches out, although, since most everyone's life was rather wretched in those days, I'm not sure why they thought witches wanted in."

Mona felt herself deflating as she stared at the elderly woman. She had been so sure Miss Kepler would be able to tell her what to do to make those women go away and stop everything from changing.

Mona mumbled her thanks as she got up. Snagging several more cookies from the tray on the table, she brooded her way to her car and home.

Chapter Twenty-Five

The preoccupation Jan had noticed in Felicity when she returned from her weekly visit to the cemetery continued over the remainder of the week and into the start of the next. Becca, Ophelia, and Jan talked about it privately, trying to intuit what it was and how they could support her.

Oddly enough, Trey had gone quiet as well. Although he and Evan still shared a brew in the evening, he no longer chatted much about his days in Totem or on the road. He would mainly sit and sing the songs of his youth. It was pleasant enough, but Evan wondered at the void of silence from him.

The women usually retreated to their own cabins following dinner and its clean-up; however, the three women decided to call on Felicity in a show of support regardless of whether she chose to take them into her confidence or not.

At the predetermined time of 7:30 p.m., they all emerged from their respective cabins and joined up to walk the very short distance to Felicity's. Ophelia knocked briskly on the door. In a moment, Felicity flung it open. Seeing the three, she immediately asked "Is something wrong?"

Ophelia pushed past her. "Yup. You." The others followed her in.

Still holding the door open, Felicity watched them settle on her loveseat and one of the two chairs. Three sets of eyes looked back at her with concern. She closed the door and crossed to the remaining chair.

"So what have I screwed up now?"

"Such a female answer," Jan chided. "Automatically assume you've done something wrong."

Becca leaned forward. "Basically, for better than a week, the body has been functioning, but the brain has been living elsewhere. You have us worried, that's all, and we wanted you to know if there's anything we can do to help, whatever it is, we're here and you just need to ask."

Felicity sat very still. This was the moment she had been wrestling with. Did she tell the others what Trey had told her or lock it away as he had done for over fifty years?

Silence stretched in the room. Finally, Felicity expelled the breath she didn't know she was holding. "Trey was at Duane's grave when I went out last week."

Becca, Ophelia, and Jan exchanged glances.

"He admitted he knew whose pickup it was that hit Duane."

"I know I wasn't around when all that happened," Jan said, "but doesn't it seem strange he didn't tell the authorities back then when they were investigating it?"

"He said he was protecting me," Felicity said.

"How did hiding the identity of the person who killed Duane help you? I would have thought having justice served would have been more beneficial," Jan responded. "Knowing that person would have to face the consequences of their actions."

Felicity closed her eyes for a moment, then opened them to stare steadily ahead. "Because it was someone connected to us. He said it was," she paused to look at Becca. "I'm so sorry, but he said it was Ike's pickup."

Becca froze as she stared back at Felicity. Then she began to shake her head. "No. No, it couldn't have been Ike. He wasn't here, remember? That's why he couldn't be a pallbearer. He had been drafted and already left for boot camp."

Ophelia snapped her fingers. "That's right. We had that bash for him. He gave Duane his old hunting rifle for safekeeping."

"Then who was driving his pickup?" Jan asked.

"My brother Ralph sold it for Ike. Figured it wouldn't be worth much if it sat around until he got out of the service," Becca answered.

"Do you remember who bought it?" Felicity asked.

Becca shook her head. "That was so long ago and I probably wasn't paying a whole lot of attention to what Ralph was doing."

Felicity sank back in the chair. "We may know the vehicle, but we still don't know the driver."

"I wonder if the DMV would have any record of it; you know, title transfer or something," Jan suggested.

"Doubtful," Ophelia said. "Things weren't computerized in those days and the truck would be long gone by now. Not likely there would be records anywhere."

An air of dejection settled over the women. Felicity's emotions whiplashed through her. So grateful that Becca's brother couldn't have been involved, but deeply disappointed they were back at the unknown.

Jan summed it up. "Somebody got really lucky in this life."

Becca felt a faint tickle at the back of her brain. She strained after it. Nothing. Dang, she wished she had Ophelia's ability to intuit things. That was a gift she never possessed. She had a moment of personal amusement as she thought how useful a Vulcan mind meld would be right now. Instead, she said, "Hey, I have a half gallon of vanilla ice cream and a hallock of strawberries that will be past their prime by tomorrow. Anyone want shakes?"

Back in her own cabin, as she blended up a pitcher full, the tickle became more of a niggle. She realized she was trying to remember something. What it was she had no clue. Of all the quirks of aging, she really hated the occasional holes in her memory. Oh well, sometimes if she just left it alone, the memory would float up. She carried the pitcher back to Felicity's where the conversation had moved onto the upcoming women's retreat.

A ginormous yawn about dislocated her jaw the next morning when Becca unlocked the door to her store. The night had proved anything but restful as her subconscious had stitched together strange dreams composed of memories and debris littering the bottom of her brain.

Ophelia dragged past her on the way to her own door. "Just so you know, I am never doing strawberry milkshakes before bed again. It felt like my mother was yammering at me all night."

"About what?" Becca asked curiously. It wouldn't be the first time that Eleanora had used her daughter to provide information to one of them.

"I dunno. She kept flipping open old ledgers or digging through old rolodexes. She was definitely busy, but about as clear as mud. All I know is I'm going to need about a gallon of coffee to make it through this day. Next stop Felicity's. What me to bring you something?"

"A quadruple shot espresso would help me remember why I'm here and what I'm doing."

Flipping on the lights, Becca hooked the carabiner with her keys to a jean belt loop and went to her computer to print out the current hunting tag information. Although it was the most profitable part of her year, it was not her favorite season. Things tended to change daily as the state constantly re-factored in fire danger, game populations, and demand.

She pulled the sheets off her printer and hauled herself out of the chair. Dropping them on the counter, she reached down to pull out the banker's box she filed the old ones in. Tucking yesterday's in a folder, she replaced the lid and then stood staring at it. Banker's box, old ledgers, rolodexes... she felt something pushing to the surface of her consciousness. It erupted simultaneously with Ophelia walking in with the coffee.

"Hey, mind watching the store a minute?" she asked Ophelia.

"With mine overrun by customers seeking help? Yeah, sure."

Stepping outside the store, Becca stopped and put her head back in. "Absolutely no lectures on the evils of hunting if anyone shows up for a tag."

"Fine, spoilsport; however, if you find someone tucked up inside one of your sleeping bags on the floor. It's me. Do not disturb."

Becca circled her cabin and unlocked the padlock to the small storage shed behind it. She always asked herself why she kept it locked. It would actually be a blessing if someone stole the junk in there. Opening the door, she stood trying to gauge just where what she was looking might be stashed. Most of what was stored were items from her family, including her two brothers, who would one day, no doubt, have a mad desire to retrieve their old Grateful Dead tee-shirts. She began shifting boxes around.

Of course, it was in the opposite corner from where she started, but she was able to find the one she was looking for. She hefted it over the stack in front of it and carried it back to her shop.

"That looks like a blast from the past," Ophelia said as Becca set the stained cardboard box with yellowed, brittle tape onto the counter.

"What it is is a long shot— a very long, long shot."

"Well, I would love to stay and watch the spiders crawl out but I have calendula to harvest and get in the drying hoop house. So now you can return my favor by watching the apothecary."

The ancient tape gave way with the lightest of tugs. The smell of the musty past drifted out of the box.

She was halfway through emptying the box when she found what she was looking for—an old manila envelope with Ike written across the front in Ralph's handwriting. Ralph loved paperwork and was a methodical record keeper, traits which made him very successful in the banking business from which he had recently retired.

She shook out the contents. It was all the records Ralph had maintained when he handled Ike's business while he was in the service. She wondered why she still kept it, as the writing on many of the papers had faded to the point of being unreadable. Unfolding still another page now fragile with age, she found what she was looking for. It was a copy of the Bill of Sale Ralph had given the purchaser of Ike's truck. She sucked in her breath sharply when she saw the name.

Her mind whirred as she pulled an envelope out of the supply by her computer, carefully slipping the sheet inside before stuffing everything else back into the box and setting it on the floor behind the counter. Should she tell

Felicity or not? She knew if she did there was going to be an explosion that the whole of Totem would feel. She decided to confer with Jan.

The two women stood on the wooden walkway outside their stores where they were able to watch all three doors. Jan was staring at Becca with her mouth agape. "Oh, wow," was all she had been able to say.

"You know what's going happen if I tell her, don't you?"

"All hell is going to break loose."

"Exactly. So do I or don't I?"

"You don't have a choice. Felicity was the one who paid the price for what happened. She lost her brother and, as a consequence, her marriage. That person's actions cost her everything while they skated scot-free. Karma's a bitch, Becca, and it just rolled around."

Becca sighed. "So the shit storm Ophelia promised us is about to blow in. I hope we all survive."

The women decided to wait to pass along the information they had uncovered until evening. After dinner, they had retreated to Becca's cabin, ostensibly to talk about the retreat. Ophelia poured everyone an iced herbal tea before joining Becca on the couch.

Accepting her glass, Felicity was puzzled. The air felt charged, counter to the sense of despondency she herself had felt since last night's great reveal had, in fact, revealed nothing.

Jan and Ophelia seemed to be nervously watching Becca, who took a couple of quick gulps from her glass before setting it on the floor beside her feet.

She cleared her throat and glanced at the other two women before pulling an envelope out of her back pocket.

"I know who bought Ike's truck."

"How? Last night you said you didn't?"

"I didn't, but something started bugging me. One of those 'you don't know but maybe you do' things. Anyway, I have a bunch of junk in my shed that goes way back. You remember how OCD Ralph was when it came to papers and stuff, so I started digging. I found this."

She handed the envelope with a copy she had made of the original Bill of Sale across to Felicity. Putting her own glass on the floor, Felicity took it.

The three women collectively held their breath as she pulled the folded sheet out and opened it.

Reading it over, Felicity went deathly still. She looked up. "Caleb? Caleb Barnwell bought Ike's truck?"

Becca nodded. "According to that, yes, he did."

Fifty plus years of pain and fury began to course through Felicity. She was actually physically vibrating. She had waited literally a lifetime for this answer. In an instant, she decided she would wait no longer.

"I think Mr. Holier-Than-Thou has had a long enough run," Felicity said through clenched teeth. She stood up and started toward the door.

"Where are you going?" Becca asked.

"To have a long overdue chat with Pastor Caleb Barnwell about souls. His."

Becca started to rise. "I'll go with…" Ophelia grabbed her arm, shaking her head. Becca sat back down as the door shut firmly behind Felicity. A few moments later they heard her car start.

"Is she going to his house?" Jan asked.

"It's Wednesday. They have services on Wednesday. She's going to the church."

"Totem won't be the same by tomorrow," Ophelia said.

Chapter Twenty-Six

Felicity arrived just as a few cars were pulling out of the church parking lot. There were lights in a room at the end of the church building and she could see people moving around. She pulled into a just-vacated parking spot. She headed to the double doors at the end of walkway and tugged at the handle. It opened. Inside, she heard a babble of voices and turned in their direction.

When Felicity stepped inside the big room, the conversation died off as everyone noticed her. Caleb was standing in the center of several people. He stared at her, his eyes hardening with contempt.

"Thou shall not suffer a witch to live," he said loudly. He expected a round of noisy approval. Silence roared in his ears instead.

Felicity advanced into the room until she was standing in front of him. "And what does the Bible says about killers, Caleb? What is their punishment?" Now a small wave of sound rolled through the room.

Dawna watched her husband. Something flicked in his face. Something like fear.

"I have no idea what you're talking about, Felicity, and this is not the time or place for discussions."

"I think you do know but let me refresh your memory. On September 12, 1969, a pickup crashed into my brother, leaving him to die on the side of the road. A pickup that had belonged to Ike Calhoun but had been sold a few months prior to someone else. You."

Her words body-slammed him. Caleb paled until his skin color faded into his short-cut white hair.

"Trey Rossiter was there. He knew Ike's pickup. Becca knew it had been sold because Ike had been drafted and found the Bill of Sale in some old family papers." She held up an envelope.

"Your brother has been dead over fifty years. Why try to make a big deal of it now?" Caleb said with a stiff smile. "It's all ancient history. It makes no difference to anyone now."

Felicity's eyes never left his face. "It made a difference every single day of my life."

Watching them both, odd little unexplained bits and pieces from her life with Caleb snapped together and Dawna knew—knew her husband had been behind the wheel that night. Caleb glanced around him. He realized people were looking at each other with uncertainty on most of their faces when he had expected to see sound condemnation. It unnerved him.

Alan Newton stepped up and held out his hand for the envelope. Felicity handed it over. Sliding the paper out, he unfolded it, reading the words on it silently. Although he said nothing, Alan's grave expression as he looked at Caleb conveyed the accuracy of Felicity's statements.

"Look, that paper could have been made anytime. Fifty years is a long time to hang onto a piece of paper. Anybody could have signed it."

Alan shook his head. "We have church records that go back almost a hundred years in the storeroom. And I happen to know Ralph's signature since he has bought insurance from me for more than forty years. And you know I know yours."

The sense of fate finally coming for him ruptured the cankerous secret hidden at his core for decades. "It was an accident," he blurted out. "I never meant to hit Duane. It was an accident."

The collective gasp sent him into a frenzy of explanation. "I was just going to hassle them; spin some gravel out from under my tires as I passed them, but the rear end of the truck fishtailed and hit Duane's bike. I saw him go down."

"And then you ran," Felicity said. "Maybe if you had gone back, gone for help, there might have been a chance Duane could have survived."

"I was scared. I had my whole life ahead of me. I was going to do good things. That could've ruined my plans, my future."

"My brother had his whole life ahead of him, too," Felicity said quietly.

When she turned to leave, Alan reached out and touched her arm. "We're here if you need us," he said as he nodded toward Bethany, who had taken up a position next to Dawna.

The smile Felicity gave him was infinitely sad. "Thanks," she whispered before making her way out of the room.

Caleb seemed to have shrunken right in front of her, Dawna thought. The self-righteous bravado that always flowed from him deeply diminished.

Around her the women began to silently clean up, before just as silently exiting. Alan was waiting at the door to the hallway having a quiet word with the other deacons as they left.

"Are you okay?" Pam asked Dawna. "Would you like me to take you home?"

"I'm okay, I think. I have my car here. Thanks, though," she answered.

"Call me if you need me," she said before leaving.

Dawna heard sobbing. Looking beyond Caleb, she saw Mona holding tissues over her mouth before she blundered out.

Then she and Caleb were the only two left. Even Alan had disappeared.

"I'll lock up," he said without looking at her.

"Okay," was all she said before exiting herself.

At home, in her bedroom, she dropped her purse and Bible on her desk. She turned slowly as she looked around. She didn't know what to think or do. Everything felt fragile, like the smallest breath of air would shatter her whole life.

She moved back to the front room and sat in the corner of the couch to wait for Caleb. She had no idea of what to say to him. What he might need from her and whether she could even provide it. A sense of the surreal encased her as she waited. Finally, she heard the door to the kitchen open and close. She heard the snick of the lock being turned and saw the light extinguish as he passed through and shut it off.

He came through the living room, not looking right or left, and not acknowledging her. In a moment, she heard the door to his office close. She got up and turned off the table lamps before heading to her own room.

***

Caleb dropped heavily into his desk chair. He was angry, maybe the angriest he had ever been. For years he had lived in fear of someone connecting him to the accident, but as the years turned into decades, he came to feel his good works absolved him; that fate held him harmless. Now it had sucker-punched him. Worse, it did so in front of much of his congregation. He was deeply disappointed in Alan Newton and the other deacons who were present. They should have run interference for him, at the least removed Felicity from the church.

It wasn't fair that at this point in his life, his career, one old woman could potentially damage everything over some punk who hadn't been worth the powder to blow him to hell. And Trey—he should have had the courtesy of dying long ago. Everybody who was around Totem back then would have figured he did. But he had jumped up like the devil himself.

Caleb drew in a deep breath and slowly let it out, trying to soothe himself. It would be okay. He was worthy. The church would stand with him and not let some far distant event besmirch his achievements. Tomorrow it would be nothing but old news. He would get everyone's attention back on the revival. By the time they held it, no one would even remember any of this. It would be okay.

***

After tossing and turning much of the night, Dawna had finally slept. The strange dream she had still clung to the back of her eyelids as she opened them to the sun already filling her room with heat. The dream floated at the front of her thoughts. She couldn't decipher it but it felt wrapped in a portentous air. She didn't like that. It made her nerves feel twitchy. She pushed back the covers and sat up.

Her mind immediately snapped back to Caleb's revelation last night. She grappled with the concept of her husband as someone who killed a man and hid it from everyone for decades. Worse than the bald facts of it was that he had not seemed to be bothered by what he had done as much as he was by being called on it. He had rushed to defend and excuse himself without any acknowledgment of the pain and destruction he had wrought on Felicity's life.

Her thoughts flitted over the numerous congregants who had witnessed the exchange. Would last night cause a change in their attitude toward Caleb? Not likely. The church people had always solidly had his back. Although she was sure there had been a lot of phoning and texting after everyone went home, things were most likely already sliding back to normal for him. But what of her? Would people assume she knew and was complicit in his perfidy?

And where did that leave her? Any trust she had in him was ruptured now. If he had hidden such a heinous act from her for fifty-plus years, what else had he hidden? She was struck by his overwhelming hypocrisy. All those times he had raised a fuss about her gnats of perceived sin while he had swallowed a camel of it. He, of course, would expect her to support him without question, but she realized she no longer had any stomach for it.

It was all just a sham; the marriage too frequently a one-way street of giving; the church with its petty judgments; even her own faith felt like it had been memorized out of a book rather than grown from her own soul.

She thought of the many stories she had absorbed through the decades about people meeting the moment that tested their mettle and helped define them. Was this hers? And, if it was, did she have the courage to meet it?

Chapter Twenty-Seven

The morning found the six deacons gathered in the insurance office. Bethany had made a pot of coffee and set out pastries she picked up at the grocery store. Then she shut herself in Alan's office space to give them privacy.

"Well, we got ourselves a mess, don't we, Alan?" Tom said as he sat his coffee on Bethany's desk before taking a healthy bite out of a bear claw.

A murmur of assent answered him.

"Any idea of what we should do?" Vic asked, his overalls already stained from the first milking of the day on his dairy farm.

Alan took a sip of his coffee. He has eschewed one of the few chairs to perch his hip on their part-time assistant's desk. He looked around at the other deacons.

"I didn't get a lot of sleep last night turning this over in my mind so please don't think I'm just shooting from the hip." He paused. "I think we need to put Caleb on a leave of absence while we wait to see what comes of this."

"Don't you think that's a bit extreme?" Vic asked. "It did happen more than a half century ago. He's done good for the church since he took over pastoring it."

Alan's face was grim. "Gentlemen, may I remind you, he killed a man. He admitted it. And, from what I saw last night, he wasn't particularly sorry about it either."

"Well, you have to admit, Duane was a wild one," Tom said.

"If I remember right, Tom, one of your sons had his wild time, too. Should he have been run down and left to bleed out on one of the backroads?"

Tom flushed. "That's true. I'm sorry. Time warps your perspective. Duane had every right to live just like my Grant. He didn't deserve to die like that."

Richard leaned forward. "There is something else. I stopped by my office to check my law books last night. What Caleb did would fall under vehicular homicide. There is no statute of limitation on taking another person's life, even accidentally, so there may be some legal ramifications as well."

Alan nodded. "Yes, that as well. Gentlemen, I am not suggesting we fire Caleb. I'm just saying, this is not some minor event we can blow by. You know, as well as I, it's all over town by now since plenty of people heard everything last night. A lot of them, both inside and outside the church, are going to be watching to see how we handle it."

"Alan's got a point. It's not only Caleb that is going to be judged, it's all of us," Richard said. "Frankly, I'm not sure I could bring the proper mindset to services being preached by a man who not only hid this from us all these years, but, according to the words coming out of his own mouth, seemingly felt justified about it."

Tom nodded. "He sure didn't show much contrition, did he? I think Alan is right. Caleb needs to step away for a while."

The other men nodded.

"So we're agreed? Okay, that brings us to the obvious issue. We would need to fill the vacancy."

"I suppose we could get one of those itinerant pastors to come in," Vic said, "but it would be hard on the budget if we have to pay two pastors. I'm guessing we would keep Caleb on the payroll since he wouldn't actually be terminated."

Their discussion was interrupted by Bethany emerging from Alan's office. "May I make a suggestion?" she said. "And sorry if I was eavesdropping, Alan's office isn't soundproof."

Alan nodded towards her. "We could use some ideas, Bet, so go ahead and share."

"I suggest you ask Dawna Barnwell to take over pastoring duties. She is fully qualified."

"I'm not sure if I understand how she is qualified, Bethany, other than being married to Caleb," Vic said.

"Dawna graduated from the same Bible college as Caleb. In fact, she was valedictorian of their class. She also went on and got her Masters of Theology. I think that qualifies her."

"Did you know this, Alan?" Tom asked.

"Not until Bethany told me about it a while back when she learned about it from Dawna during one of the women's meetings."

"Funny, Caleb didn't mention his wife's qualifications when we had that chat about her starting a women's ministry. In fact, he kinda hinted she wasn't qualified at all." Tom said. "Seems like he has been keeping all the glory for himself."

"It would solve a lot of problems if Dawna would be willing to give it a try. It would buy us time to see which way the wind is going to blow on this whole thing, and we could give Caleb's salary to Dawna so nothing would change financially, including their own economic status," Richard pointed out.

"She might not be interested," Vic said. "Might make it awkward at home."

"We won't know until we ask," Alan said.

Chapter Twenty-Eight

The same morning was busier than usual at the deli as Felicity had become an item of interest based on the town's gossip tree. She sent Enoch to fetch Jan to help out. In addition to filling coffee cups and bagging muffins, Jan also stood guardian against the few whose actions indicated deep disapproval of the situation. They huffed and puffed through giving and receiving their order, but Jan's brown eyes sent hard warnings any discourtesy would be dealt with swiftly and not by Felicity.

By mid-morning the traffic had died down to its usual level.

"Well, at least they didn't show up en masse with pitchforks and flaming torches," Jan noted as she rounded the counter into the main part of the room, preparing to head back to her own store.

"I appreciate the help and you backing down the old biddies with a craw full of venom. I probably would have punched one of them in the throat if they had started in on me."

"Blast my good intentions. I would have loved to see that even if it doesn't exactly align with Summerland's philosophy," Jan said as she left.

The rest of the morning disappeared into Felicity's food prep and then the lunch hour when more of Totem came to gather a sandwich and a look at her. She suspected one or two would have liked to chastise her, but with Trey and Evan in the corner eating their french dips and Enoch at the kitchen sink, they just gave her thin-lipped non-smiles and left with their white bags.

At mid-afternoon, everything stilled. Felicity poured herself a cup of coffee and, after wiping the counter one more time, went to sit in the chair favored by Trey. The whole event had opened a new grief in her. She had always believed learning who killed Duane would bring some kind of solace. Instead, she felt another kind of bereavement at the recognition there would be no justice served up to Duane. Too many years had passed. It was now nothing but a brief ripple in Totem. Tomorrow it would flatten out and disappear entirely. Caleb would go on being sanctimonious with the full support of his church. The greatest punishment he would face for stealing her brother's life was the bit of embarrassment she may have caused him last night. She nearly gave way to the tears building behind her eyes when a customer came through the door.

Turning, she was surprised to see Dawna heading straight for her. Slipping into the chair opposite her, Dawna reached out and grasped Felicity's hand. "I had a pretty little speech all prepared but I don't know if any words are adequate so all I can offer is I am here for you in whatever way you might have need of."

Felicity nodded her acknowledgement of the kindness. "Thank you." She was quiet a moment before looking Dawna in the eyes. "I know you weren't here when it happened, but did Caleb ever tell you about it?"

Dawna shook her head. "No. I had no more idea than anyone else. There were a few stray remarks made over the years, but I had nothing to connect them with so they were just kind of meaningless to me."

Felicity looked out the window. "It's been so long, there isn't much that can be done now. At least I kept my promise to Duane. I found out who stole his life. Now, it will be up to the universe what happens."

Dawna's face was deeply troubled. "Truthfully, I have no idea if there will be any repercussions from the church. Caleb has always been able to manipulate most situations in his favor. I'm guessing this one will be no different."

"That's not your fault."

"Maybe some of it is. I have been such a milquetoast; always taking the coward's way in the interest of maintaining the peace."

"Every day we have a chance to do things differently."

"The infamous second chance. Or, in my case, the thousandth."

Felicity's smile was faint. "You only need to one to change course."

Dawna sank back in the chair. "Can you really do that at our age? I feel like I've walked myself so deep in a rut that I can't even see over the edge."

"Who do you want to be?"

"Not Caleb's perfect little helpmate!" she snapped out before looking at Felicity, startled for a moment. "Wow, where did that come from?"

"From the woman you have kept silenced for too long. Maybe you and she should have a conversation. I think that woman knows exactly what you need."

Before Dawna could respond, her cell phone sounded. She pulled it out of her purse and tapped through to a text message. After reading it, she quickly replied before slipping it back into her purse. "That's odd. The deacons want me to come to the church tonight for a special meeting they're having. I never am invited to those things." She looked at Felicity, mystified.

Staring back, Felicity drew in a deep breath of air carrying cigarette smoke on it. Regardless of her skepticism, apparently the universe was moving and it wanted something from her.

Her own phone rang before she could focus on the feeling Eleanora's presence had evoked in her. It was Bethany.

"Hey, girl, I need a couple of those fantastic roast beef sandwiches of yours along with a couple of sides of potato salad. Alan's got a meeting tonight and I don't have to cook. Woohoo! Can I pick them up about 3:45? And I just might have some news for you."

"Good, I hope," Felicity said.

"I think it just might be. Oh, and please don't say anything about it to anyone. It's still undercover."

"I won't. Two roast beefs it is"

Clicking off, she smiled at the woman across from her. "Thank you for coming by, Dawna. It couldn't have been easy considering it might appear as a failure to 'stand by your man' situation so I appreciate it very much."

Dawna's tone was crisp. "Anything and everything that comes from this is on him. You were the one true victim. You are the only one that deserves any comfort I can give." For a moment the hidden woman inside Dawna looked out at Felicity. Then Dawna colored slightly and the woman disappeared. "You know, I doubt Caleb will have time for a regular dinner tonight if the deacons are meeting, so I think I would like a couple of sandwiches with a side of your broccoli salad for each, please. Chicken salad if you have it."

Felicity sighed inwardly as she got up to prep the food for Dawna. The woman seemed to have no idea of the power she kept suppressing. She literally could not conceive she already held the key to everything she was desperately looking for.

***

Felicity bent down to retrieve Bethany's order from the small dorm fridge under the counter when she saw her opening the door.

Stopping before she reached the counter, Bethany looked around. "Anyone here but us?" she asked.

Felicity shook her head. "Nope. Enoch is down helping Ophelia match lids to the containers she ordered."

"Good," Bethany said as she came up and slid onto one of the counter stools, "because this is just for your ears only, at least until later tonight." She leaned across the counter conspiratorially. "Tonight the deacons are going to put Caleb on a leave of absence. And…" she paused for effect, "they are going to ask Dawna to take over as the interim pastor."

Felicity's eyes widened. "Seriously?"

Bethany nodded. "Absolutely. They held a meeting this morning at our office. I wasn't part of most of it, but I was sitting in Alan's office and heard it all. It really galled them that Caleb not only caused Duane's accident, he apparently justified it by thinking his life mattered more. Anyway, that's the lay of the land right now. Caleb is not going to take this well so I'll fill you in on all the messy details tomorrow. I just hope that Dawna has the guts to step up. It's going to make it hard for the church if they have to try to pay two pastors and I personally think she would do a great job. Anyway, Alan's waiting. How much do I owe you?"

Felicity blindly stared out the window at the parking lot as Bethany left. Dawna needed guts? Dawna would get guts and everyone would be getting sandwiches for dinner. Summerland had work to do this evening. She spun around and reached for the bread.

At four o'clock, she lifted the box she had stacked all the white bags in, and, after doing a quick check to make sure everything was off, headed to the door, locking it behind her.

Her destination was next door at Jan's shop. Raised in the southwest, Jan was an aficionado of heat and her shop door stood open to the afternoon's intense warmth. Jan looked up from her beading tray when Felicity sat the box on the counter, grabbing two bags off the top.

"We have a mission this evening that's going to need some prep work so it's fast food for everyone. We'll meet at Ophelia's at five."

"Does Ophelia know this?"

"Not yet. I'm going to drop these off for Evan and Trey. This doesn't suit them, they can head into town for something else."

"You're sounding a bit fierce."

"Actually, fierce might be an understatement," Felicity said as she headed out the door.

While the women were eating their sandwiches and salads, Felicity outlined what Bethany had relayed to her.

"So what are we going to do about it?" Becca asked.

"We are going to do a circle for Dawna," Felicity said.

"Ummm, you know it's forbidden to try influence someone's own will," Jan said, crumpling the sandwich wrapper.

"We are not going to influence her will. Dawna has everything already in her—locked down tight. We are simply going to provide a little oil for that lock so she can make the decision that is right and true for her."

Ophelia flattened her sandwich bag and dug in her pocket for a pen. "So what herbs do you think we need?" she asked, pen poised.

"Definitely skullcap," Felicity said. "I totally doubt that Caleb is going to be happy with this and will look for a target, which puts Dawna right in the crosshairs in many ways. She'll need protection against him."

Ophelia jotted it down. "You said she needs a courage boost, so nettle. Okay, we have fire and water."

"How about mugwort for earth?" Becca suggested. "It will help ground her so she can work from her truest core."

"And sage for air," Jan said, "so she has the wisdom she needs to make the choice that's best for her."

Felicity nodded. "That should cover all the probable bases. So we have time to purify, and get set up. Dawna told me the deacons wanted to meet with her at 6:30. Let's start about 6:15."

The other women voiced their assent and scattered.

***

The few pieces of charcoal Becca had lit were already turning grey in the fire ring when Ophelia plunked the small cauldron on top. She carried four small wooden dishes and a wand poked out of her jeans' back pocket. She moved around the circle, placing a dish on the small wooden log benches that marked the directions.

In a moment, Jan and Felicity joined them. Like Becca and Ophelia, they wore a peasant-style top in a color representing their particular element. The yoke and cuffs beaded with symbols delicately outlining an aspect of the element.

Each took position in front of a bench, facing outward. They stood for a quiet moment, aligning themselves with their intent and each other. Then Jan raised her wand. "Element of air, I call on you." In turn, Felicity called in fire, Ophelia water, and Becca earth.

With the circle of protection called into place, the women turned to face the cauldron. One by one they added the contents of the dishes to the cauldron, speaking their purpose in supporting Dawna. When all the herbs had been placed in the pot, they sat quietly keeping their intentions focused.

Chapter Twenty-Nine

After arriving at home, Dawna automatically placed the bag she had gotten at the deli in the refrigerator, her mind puzzling over the odd request to meet with the deacons. She thought about contacting Bethany to see if she knew what was going on but decided against it. Considering her long experience in the church, it was, no doubt, something to do with the revival. She poured herself a glass of ice water and went to her room to freshen up.

She was glad about her dinner decision when Caleb texted her he was meeting with the deacons at 6:00 so he was just going to grab something beforehand. It also confirmed her guess that everything was going to continue along in the church as it always had.

In the time between her homecoming and leaving again for the church, she found a growing sense of disappointment and moral outrage spreading through her. Was the church really going to brush Caleb's actions under the rug? A young man had died because of both his actions and his inability to see anyone's needs other than his own. Suddenly she felt an aversion to the place she had been part of for so many years. It felt like a place where man was no longer made in God's image, but God had come to be formed in man's image. Or more specifically, Caleb's image.

Dawna pulled into the parking lot a few minutes before the designated time. She was surprised to see Bethany sitting on the small bench outside the doors to the offices and fellowship hall.

Bethany stood up at her approach. "Hey there. We're supposed to hide out in Pam's office until they're done meeting with Caleb."

"Okay," Dawna said. "So what's going on? I hate to sound suspicious, but this is a bit out of the usual."

Bethany hooked her arm through Dawna's and steered her to Pam's office, closing the door behind them. "Sorry, but my lips are sealed. My mission is to hang with you until they're ready."

As they stepped into Pam's office, Dawna could hear raised voices coming from the fellowship hall. Were the men arguing?

It was closer to 6:45 when she heard the fellowship hall door bang open and, a moment later, the outside door slam. Alan opened the door. "Hi, Dawna, I think we're ready now."

Dawna followed him and was surprised not to see Caleb in his usual place at the head of the table. A couple of the men were standing off to one side and there was a distinct air of tension in the room. It felt as if something unpleasant had occurred.

"Sit here, Dawna," Alan said as he indicated the chair usually held by Caleb. "Gentlemen, I think we're ready." Tom and Vic returned to the table while Alan took up position at the end opposite of her. They were all looking at her gravely. It set off a queasy feeling in her stomach.

"Dawna," Alan nodded around the table, "in light of the information that was disclosed last night, we made the determination to place Caleb on a leave of absence. How long is yet to be determined."

For a moment, it felt like her heart literally stopped as she stared at them. Caleb banished?

"I know it may feel harsh given the amount of time that has passed since the event, but it is hard for us to reconcile his position in the church with his seeming indifference to the significance of what he did."

Something steadied in her. "Yes. I understand," she said quietly. For a moment, it was as if something warm and safe wrapped around her.

"So essentially we now have a pastoral vacancy needing to be filled. According to Bethany, you graduated from Bible college and also attained a Master's in Theology, if I remember correctly."

Dawna nodded. "Yes. Caleb and I met when we were both at the Bible college. While he was serving as an itinerant pastor, I completed my Master's."

"Would you consider stepping in as our fill-in pastor while we sort out this situation?"

It felt as though every cell in her body expanded and lunged toward the offer. Almost immediately, her mind began to try to suck them back, quickly racking up excuses to stay in the safe background she had always inhabited. Then Felicity's voice skittered across her brain. You only need one. And with it a geyser of something that felt like her but bigger, bolder.

"Yes. I would be very much willing to fill in, under one condition, if I might. That I'm allowed to take my own direction and not just act as a pseudo-Caleb."

The moment the words were out of her mouth, she sat back, stunned at herself.

There was silence from the men, then Tom broke it. "Frankly, I think we need some change around here. Liv and I have felt that some of the congregation has been getting short shrift for a long time so I'm okay with something new. Gents?" he said as he looked around the table.

The men were nodding with varying degrees of enthusiasm.

"We are agreed then to Dawna's request? Okay, that leaves one elephant in the room. What about the revival?"

"Cancel it." Dawna's voice was firm.

"It's not that simple. There is some economic impact to the church. It does bring in a tidy sum every year and we have deposits we would lose," Richard pointed out.

"Then let's cancel the format and do something more inclusive."

"Such as?" Vic asked.

Dawna shook her head. "Not sure now, but I bet the women can figure it out."

For one brief, unsettling moment, the men felt the ground shift beneath them. But just as quickly, they manned up and agreed.

After Alan announced he would put a notification on the church web page and send a text message to notify the parishioners of the change, Dawna was free to leave. Settling in her car, she wondered at herself. She hadn't acted so sure of herself since…since she was class president in Bible college. It was like someone unfamiliar, yet familiar, had taken control. But she welcomed the her that had stepped into view. That emerging woman had just opened vistas she couldn't have imagined this morning.

Chapter Thirty

Mona's whole body began to shake as a shriek of anguish rolled through her. She stared at the cell phone screen in her hand; she read and reread the message from the deacons, trying to tease out what the real meaning of the announcement that Pastor Barnwell would be taking a leave of absence from the church and that his wife would be assuming pastoral duties effective as of today.

Setting the phone down, she grabbed up the bag of potato chips she had been eating when the beep alerted her to the message. She began to rapidly cram them into her mouth.

It was that witch woman who had come to the church after Wednesday service. She had accused Pastor of doing something terrible. That proved it. Those women were behind all the things that were making the church upset. Mona knew this for a fact because she had been the one who had seen Mrs. Barnwell with that woman.

She had to stop it. She had to stop the witches. She tried to remember what Miss Kepler had told her a couple of weeks ago. Something about buried iron and witch balls. She didn't understand. Then she remembered. Burning. Miss Kepler said they used to burn witches. She wasn't sure how she would do that. She couldn't actually burn them, but maybe if she burned their stuff, they would go away.

She needed paper and pencil. Years ago, one of her teachers in high school had taught her to write down what she had to do to complete her projects. Otherwise she got things mixed up and missed whole pieces. She needed to do that so she didn't mess up the mission she had just assigned herself. She got up, stepping on the potato chip bag, its remains crunching under her foot as she went to hunt for the notebook she used at Bible study and dig a pen out of her purse.

At the top of a blank page, she wrote Get Rid of Witches in her childish scrawl. She sat struggling to figure out what she should do. Then a movie she had seen years ago when her aunt was still alive floated up in her mind. There were people who were trying to get rid of something evil and they had it trapped in an old house. They dressed in black and then sneaked up with gas cans, splashing it all round before throwing a lighted match and running away. The evil thing went away when the house burned. That memory would be her road map.

She wrote down black clothes. She had the pants and the black blouse she bought to wear to her aunt's funeral. She didn't like black much so she had never worn it again. She wrote them down as well.

Then she wondered about where she would get something like gas to make the fire. Chewing on the pen, she remembered there were a couple of small cans of kerosene in the little shed out back. Her aunt had a kerosene heater she used to use. Mona hated the smell of it so she would never light it after she came to help her aunt. She wrote the word kerosene down under black clothes.

She would need something to light the kerosene. She thought about the long lighters that were in the drawer at the church. The men had used them to ignite the barbeques when they had their annual picnic. She would get one of them tomorrow when she was at the church. She wrote it on the paper and sat back.

There, she had everything she needed to get rid of the witches. She felt very pleased with herself. Once they were gone, Pastor Barnwell could come back to the church and everything would go back to the way it was supposed to be.

Chapter Thirty-One

Caleb was waiting for her when she got home.

"So you think you can replace me," he threw at her the moment she came through the door.

Dawna calmly set her purse on the kitchen island before facing him. "No. I have no intention of replacing you. What I am doing is stepping up to temporarily fill in until things settle and final decisions are made regarding the situation, which, incidentally, you created."

"It was a stupid accident, that's all. People have accidents every day. They don't get kicked out of their jobs for it."

"It wasn't a fender-bender. A young man lost his life because of your 'accident'. And maybe the problem isn't so much the actual accident, but rather your inability to see the cost, not only to the man you killed, but to other people who are still breathing, and own up to it."

"Why should I? Felicity doesn't belong to our church. I have no obligation to her."

Dawna's nostrils flared as she drew in a deep breath. "Then you have missed the whole point of being a Christian."

Caleb stared at his wife as she stared back. For the first time, he felt real fear begin to crawl around in his midsection as he realized his carefully cultivated pastoral persona was being called into question even by his wife. He had spent many a sermon exhorting his congregants about preparing for a coming judgment day. Was it coming now for him?

Chapter Thirty-Two

Mrs. Barnwell was already in the pastor's office the next morning when Mona arrived at the church. Although she gave her a good morning greeting, Mona ignored her as she headed to the cupboard in the kitchen to retrieve her tote of cleaning supplies. Peering over her shoulder to ensure no one was watching, Mona opened the drawer with the lighters. She pulled one out and slipped it into the pocket of her smock. She smiled happily as she picked up her tote. It wouldn't be long and everything would go back to the way it had always been. She would make that happen.

Mona gobbled the corn dogs and macaroni salad she had picked up at the deli section of Seb's grocery store. Then she hurried into the bedroom and dug around in the piles of clothes littering the floor and furniture until she found the black blouse and pants. After changing, she added her black tennis shoes. Looking over the top of the debris mounded on her dresser, she was pleased that she looked like the people from the movie.

She went back to the front room to consult her list. Kerosene. She needed to put the kerosene in her car along with the lighter.

She pushed aside the old grocery bags, and empty pop cans in the trunk to put the two cans in. Only one of the cans was full. The other was pretty light. She hoped she had enough. Back inside, she fished her keys out of her purse before dropping the lighter in. Now she could go.

Backing out of her driveway, she headed to Hag Hallow. She slowed and started to pull in when she saw several cars in the parking lot and one of the men walking from the building toward the little cabins. She slammed on her brakes hard as she realized it was still light out. No, no. It had to be dark. The witches would see her and escape. She turned around and headed back to her house. She had to wait. It had to be dark just like in the movie.

Mona awoke with a start. She had dozed off waiting for the light to fade. Peering out the window, she realized it was dark. Her phone said it was 1:18 a.m. Now it was right. She retraced her drive.

She nosed her car into the parking lot drive before stopping to peer at the darkness edging the parking lot. After watching a few minutes, she didn't see anyone or any movement indicating someone was lurking in the shadows. She drove in before carefully turning around to point her car in the direction of the road. After opening the trunk, she stood still, listening hard for any noise that might be made by a person. It was silent other than the night sounds of the woods around her. She picked up the full can and climbed up to the walk area. Starting in front of the deli, she began to splash it around on the boards. She was disappointed when she ran out just past the window before the art place. Returning to her car, she retrieved the other can. Although she tried to stretch it as far as she could while splashing it over the steps, she didn't even make it all the way to the apothecary door before the can was empty.

Tossing it back in her car, she carefully closed the trunk lid and then crawled into the driver's seat to reach her purse with the lighter. She touched the flame to the kerosene on the walk, then the stairs. She was fascinated as the flame eagerly began to gobble the fuel. Staring at it, the smoke swirled up until it looked like a tall, thin woman walking through the fire toward her. Panicked, she headed to her car as fast as her girth allowed. She literally spun gravel out from under her wheels as she accelerated out of the parking lot.

Chapter Thirty-Three

Rolling over in his sleep, Evan thought he heard someone call his name. He searched his dreamscape looking for the source when it came again. This time his subconscious recognized it was coming from outside him and pushed him to consciousness. He sat up abruptly hearing his name again. The voice was close and unfamiliar, but the urgency in it made him grab for his jeans and tee-shirt. Thrusting his feet into his shoes, he quickly crossed the small area of the cabin, unlocking and throwing his door open. Stepping onto the porch, he caught the smell of smoke and saw the glimmer of fire coming from the storefront.

He broke into a run, pausing only to grab the sand-filled bucket beside the steps the women kept for people to douse their cigarettes. Throwing the contents over the flames in front of Jan's door, he stepped back and scooped up another bucket of sand and gravel from the parking lot and threw it.

He heard Enoch's voice come timidly out of the shadows. "Mister?"

Evan called to him. "Enoch, get the ladies!"

The man didn't answer but Evan heard what sounded like the scrabble of gravel from the steps up to their cabins. He immediately dragged more gravel into the bucket and tossed it.

"Shit, man," rumbled in his ears. Trey loomed upside him. "Got another bucket?"

"Other end of the porch," Evan said jerking his head in the direction of the east side.

Trey made for it and tossed the contents over the flames licking at the deli door. He, too, stepped back to scoop up gravel and dirt from the parking lot, flinging it at the flames.

Becca was the first to appear. After stopping at the end of the walkway closest to her shop, she turned and headed back to her cabin. She returned in a few moments with a fire extinguisher in her hand. She handed it off to Jan, who arrived just before Felicity and Ophelia. Jan pulled the pin and aimed it at the flames in front of the apothecary while Becca quickly climbed to her door and after fumbling for a moment, pushed it open, automatically flipping on the lights. She exited carrying several fire extinguishers in her arms. The women crowded around her grabbing for the devices while Evan and Trey continued to throw dirt.

The flames were slowly choking out when flashing lights and sirens let them know the town's small fire department was approaching. They all moved back when the engine and water tender pulled into the parking lot. Instantly, several people in turnouts jumped out of the truck, grabbing large extinguishers from compartments in the side of the fire engine.

When there was only scorched wood and stained foam left, the fire chief and another fireperson began to run their high-powered flashlights back and forth, leaning in to closely examine the scene. They walked back and forth several times before the chief shut off his light and headed in the direction of the group clustered at the end of the building.

The women stepped up to meet him. He shoved his helmet up as he greeted them. "Well, gals, you are the victims of somebody's poor attempt at arson. Thankfully, they used an inadequate amount of kerosene; enough to cause some damage but, obviously, not enough to burn your building to the ground. Who discovered the fire?"

Evan moved into line with the women. "I did, sir."

"Did you see or hear anything that brought it to your attention?"

Evan remembered the voice. Fortunately the darkness hid the embarrassment of his admission. "No. Someone called my name and when I went to see who it was, I spotted the fire."

"Who called you?" the chief asked.

Evan's embarrassment deepened. "I never saw anyone, just heard a voice." He waited for the disbelief. The only thing forthcoming was a sigh. "Doesn't surprise me given it's this place," was all the chief said.

At that moment, something fell against Evan's back. He twisted just in time to catch Trey as he was collapsing. The fire chief stepped around him to grab the man's other arm. Together they slowly lowered him to the ground.

"It's his heart," Evan said as the chief called out for one of the firemen to bring the medic bag.

Trey weakly raised his hand. "No," he said in a hoarse whisper. "It's the end of the road. I'm just gonna ride on out." His hand fell.

From the bag dropped beside him, the chief pulled out a stethoscope and applied it to Trey's chest. After moving it around several times, he pulled the earpieces out and shook his head.

Tears surprised Evan when they stung his eyes. He looked up over the shoulder of the fire chief to the path leading to the cabins as he tried to quell them. He was startled to see a tall young man in vintage clothes standing there; his face indistinct. In a moment, he saw another man walk into view. Although this man also looked young, Evan recognized Trey's way of moving. The two faced each other for a moment before flinging their arms around each other's shoulders, fading from view as they headed down the path.

Felicity squatted beside Evan, reaching out to take Trey's hand. "Safe journey, old friend." She held it for a moment before gently resting it on his chest. When she stood up, Ophelia and Becca moved in to wrap their arms around her, steering her toward the cabins.

When only Jan and Evan remained, the chief quietly spoke. "I'll call the funeral home unless you think an autopsy is in order."

"He told us his heart was giving out when he returned to Totem," Jan said. "He said he wanted to die here."

Evan nodded his concurrence. "We spent a lot of time together in the past couple of months. He was struggling more and more each day."

One of the firemen brought a blanket and carefully covered Trey's body. The chief asked if one or both of them would stay with the body until the hearse arrived. They nodded their agreement. He turned to leave before turning back. "The police will be coming to talk to you about the fire. My grandmother was a friend of Eleanora's so I've pretty much known my whole life about the, ahh…" he paused. "unusual things that occur in these here parts. He's a newcomer so maybe you were getting up to go to the bathroom when you spotted the fire."

Evan and Jan stood shoulder to shoulder as they watched the fire trucks back out of the driveway and turn towards town.

The hearse pulled in ahead of the police car. Evan helped the funeral director place Trey in the body bag and lift him onto the gurney. The officer stayed respectfully away by tying yellow police scene tape around the perimeter of the porch. Only when the hearse had pulled out did he approach Evan and Jan. He did little more than ask them to not touch anything until later in the day, indicating the department's chief would come out after daylight to take pictures and talk to everyone then.

***

Social media spread the news of the attempted arson throughout Totem by morning. After getting only a bit more sleep, Evan stationed himself at the front of the building to make sure curious community members driving in for a look didn't approach the scene. Enoch joined him, staring confusedly at the taped-off building.

"Broked?" he asked

Evan smiled at him reassuringly. "Yes. But we can fix it. You can help me."

Enoch's face lit up. "Help Mister?"

Evan nodded. "Yes. Help Mister."

Becca arrived with a cup of coffee and a breakfast sandwich. After handing them over to Evan, she put her arm around Enoch. "No work," she said. "Play day."

"Play?"

"Yes. Play."

Enoch grinned and immediately trotted towards his camp trailer. "He and his stuffies will hang out in front of cartoons the rest of the day," Becca said. "He has about sixty of them. They're his family."

"How's Felicity?" Evan asked.

"She's sitting with her grief. Trey was her last real link to her brother and the promise of a future that never happened. When he came back, he brought the past into the present. Now he has taken it again. So in a sense, she's lost both all over."

Evan looked down the path. "I don't know if it would be of any comfort to her, but maybe Trey and her brother have connected on the other side."

Becca arched a questioning eyebrow at him.

"Okay, this is going to sound like I've lost it, but right at the moment Trey passed. I thought I saw someone, a tall guy with long dark hair wearing really vintage clothes down there on the path. Then another tall man with long dark hair showed up. I couldn't see his face but he moved in that loose way Trey did. They threw their arms around each other's shoulders and then just walked into nothingness." He paused. "Okay, you can commit me any time."

Becca's grin was mischievous. "Ummm, so now you are seeing beyond the veil. Sounds like Summerland has seeped in pretty deep. Guess maybe you're just gonna have stay on." She eyed the damaged porch and steps. "And maybe because apparently somebody really doesn't like us."

Chapter Thirty-Four

Pam brought in a cup of tea while Dawna was sorting through the numerous papers on Caleb's desk, slipping them into file folders. Taking a grateful sip from the cup proffered to her, she waved at one of the two stacks of folders. "That one has what looks like Caleb's personal notes, sermons, etc. so I'm going to store them in the file cabinet and that pile appears to be all related to church business and finances. Maybe you could help me go through things and decide what's important, what isn't, and what's redundant that I could get rid of."

"Happy to. Caleb had this thing about hanging on to every piece of paper that he touched. So did you hear about the fire last night at Hag Hallow? Apparently, somebody tried to burn the women's businesses down."

"Good Lord, how bad was it? Is everyone okay?"

"From what people have posted on Facebook, it was mainly the stairs and walkway that were damaged, although, apparently, the man who used to be married to Felicity way back when had a heart attack and died fighting it."

Before Dawna could reply, they heard a small screech at the door to the office. Mona stood in the doorway shaking her head back and forth. "No, no. You need to go away. Pastor Barnwell is supposed to be here so everything can be like it always was before the witches. I made them go away. I did everything right, just like in the movie. Witches have to be burned, you know."

Dawna and Pam exchanged horrified looks. Moving her hand to signal Pam to make a call, Dawna spoke soothingly to Mona. "Pastor Barnwell had to go to the Valley to check on things for the revival, Mona. He asked me to help clear up his desk for him. He'll be back in a while."

Pam took the clue. "And that reminds me, I better call on those chairs like he asked me to. He won't be happy if we don't have enough chairs," she said as she crossed the room and slipped past Mona.

Dawna smiled what she hoped was a reassuring smile. "Nothing to worry about, Mona, except making sure the church is clean for the Sunday service."

Letting out a relieved sigh, Mona headed to the nave.

Dawna was collapsed back in her chair when Pam returned. "They're on their way," she said quietly.

"I'll wait for them outside," Dawna said.

It was a hard half hour as Dawna explained Mona's neurodivergence to the chief and woman officer who had shown up. They handled the situation deftly. Mona was delighted to explain to them about her efforts to free the church from the grasp of the witches who were making trouble for everyone. When asked, she led the officers out to open the trunk to her car and show them the kerosene cans. She wasn't alarmed when the woman officer invited her to come to the station so they could write down her efforts to save the church.

The chief stopped to tell Dawna and Pam they would be sending a tow truck to collect Mona's car. "This is going to be a tough one," he said. "She obviously has some serious issues. So who do we need to notify about her situation?"

"As far as I know the church is the only family she has," Pam said.

"Going to be hard to stand by her after this," the chief said.

Dawna lifted her chin. "No, it won't. I don't condone anything Mona did, but we won't abandon her either. She's going to need a lot of support because I'm not sure she'll ever understand why what she did was genuinely wrong when it was so right in her mind."

The chief shook his head. "This has been a strange one. I was actually just heading out to investigate the fire when your call came in. First time I ever solved a case before I even saw the crime scene."

***

Watching the cruisers clear the parking lot, Dawna spoke quietly. "Mona may have been the one who acted but I can't help but feel the church was complicit."

Pam nodded. "I think we blew off warning signs because it was easier than digging in and trying to help her understand the things that frightened her to the point where she tried to stop them herself."

Back inside the church, Pam asked if there was anything she could do to help as she watched distress deepen on Dawna's face.

Dawna shook her head. "I think I just need a few minutes to process it," she said as she turned towards the doors leading to the nave.

The lights were on as Mona had already started to clean. Dawna flicked them off before sitting in a shadowed pew. As she stared through the dimness at the large wooden cross affixed to the wall behind the pulpit, the dream she had several nights ago rose to the front of her thoughts. In it, she had walked on bleached land. In the center was a single tree, twisted and spindly that seemed to suck any nutrition into itself, leaving little for the other stunted and ill-looking plants spotted around it. She had been unable to decipher its meaning when she had it, but now understanding came. She was seeing the church, perhaps as the heavens saw it. Far from being a thriving enterprise ripe with the fruits of the spirit described in the Bible, it was starved and dying. She realized how very blind she had been to the actual state of things versus what she had chosen to believe they were.

She knew what Caleb's first reaction would have been to today's events. He would be running around with a cloth of words wiping away any responsibility the church had for Mona's actions. She would not do that. It wasn't going to be comfortable but she needed to go to Summerland and see what might be done to rectify some of the mayhem the church had set loose.

Chapter Thirty-Five

The only business without damaged stairs and steps was the outdoor store. Jan, Becca, and Ophelia had gathered inside to give their statements to the police. Evan, following the fire chief's advice, had already given his and, having been excused, gone to the cabin Trey had occupied. He smiled sadly to himself when he stepped inside. The cabin was helter-skelter and so reflective of the man himself. He was looking for the saddlebags which Trey had said contained the cremation plan.

He found them half-kicked under the bed. Flipping open the flap on one side, he found a couple of small notebooks, and scraps of envelopes and paper. The other side had a thick envelope with the name of the cremation company on the corner.

Carefully shutting the door behind him, he headed to the cabins. Felicity's was the last of the women's small structures. He knocked lightly on the door, opening it when she called out to come in.

She was sitting on the loveseat, cradling a cup of coffee in her hands. Although her damp hair evidenced a recent shower and her clothes were fresh, she still retained an air of being faintly stunned.

Evan crossed to sit in the armchair before holding out the envelope. "Trey told me some time ago he had purchased a cremation plan. I found it where he said it would be. My understanding was they would take care of all the final arrangements for him."

Felicity stared at the envelope but made no attempt to take it from Evan.

"If you want, I'll contact them and get it handled."

"I hate to put that on you. Trey wasn't part of your responsibilities."

"He became my friend these last few months and he entrusted me to do a couple of things for him when he passed. This is one. The other is he wanted to be buried with your brother."

Felicity smiled faintly. "He would. It was like they were each half of a single soul."

"I don't want to overstep any boundaries, but I would like to handle that—for you and… and him."

"You're a good man, Evan, and I would be grateful if you would." Her eyes drifted back to the window.

Evan quietly left.

He had just reached the parking lot when a neat compact car pulled in and parked on the opposite side of the lot. The woman who exited it looked vaguely familiar, but then he had seen so many people who frequented the deli and the other shops that he recognized many people who were, in fact, strangers to him.

She took several steps in the direction of the building before pausing and staring at it.

Evan walked to her. "I'm sorry, but there has been a fire and everything is closed."

A brief smile came and went on her face. "Yes, I know. Could you tell me where Felicity is?"

"She's in her cabin, but I'm not—" but the woman was already heading toward them. He shrugged. She obviously knew Felicity,

Dawna stopped and drew a deep breath before knocking on the door. When Felicity answered the door, she was startled to see Dawna waiting on her stoop. She motioned her in.

Dawna sat on the edge of the same chair Evan had previously occupied, shaking her head when Felicity offered her tea. "No, thank you. I came to tell you I know who started the fire last night and that the police have already taken her into custody and I am so, so sorry that we let things get to the point this happened."

"I'm not sure I'm following what you are saying."

Dawna took a deep breath and then carefully outlined the events leading to last night's events. "I feel a deep responsibility for the situation," she said.

"I'm not sure why. You had no way of knowing Mona was slipping off the tracks."

"I knew she had become obsessed with the idea that you and the other women were witches. She was always bringing it up after one of our other church members inadvertently planted the idea in her mind. The rest of us just tended to blow it off, thinking she would come to realize it was just idle gossip and she should forget about it. We didn't pay enough attention to recognize it had become quite real for her and that she felt a compulsion to act on it, although I wouldn't have guessed she had the capability to put even a rudimentary plan together, let alone actually try to execute it."

"Thank you. All of us will sleep a bit better tonight since we now know the genesis of that fire. And, I understand you've taken over pastoring the church. Congratulations."

"Today I realized just how obviously unprepared I am to do that."

Felicity's brows drew together. "But you studied for it, right?"

Dawna eased back in the chair. "I spent about six years studying, with great emphasis on interpreting the Bible, leadership classes galore, liturgy, even counseling. But it feels like everything was aimed at helping other people conform to learning to believe a certain way. Basically, molding someone to fit the church when, maybe, the focus should be molding the church to fit the needs of a person."

"In other words, dogma versus an open-mindedness about individual situations."

"Exactly."

"Isn't there something in the Bible about scales falling from eyes?"

"It's in Acts."

"I believe that the scales are falling from your eyes. You're beginning to see a wider picture."

"Yes, but then what?"

Felicity leaned forward. "I have a feeling that your church is going to need a serious overhaul. Right now, it has been entirely molded to fit one man's vision of what it should be."

Dawna nodded. "That's true enough."

"But for you to reshape it, you're going to have to take off your goody-goody shoes and put on your bad-ass bloomers."

Dawna's eyes widened. "My what?"

"You yourself have told me you've been too mild; that you've always taken the safe road rather than risk stirring things up, even when it went against the grain of your soul. It seems to me with all that's happened in the last few weeks, the universe is telling you to be more than you've allowed yourself to be for decades. You're going to have to ruffle feathers to get the flock shaped up."

"I don't feel comfortable with that. That's not the image of a good Christian woman."

Felicity rolled her eyes. "Dawna, did you ever stop to think how many women in the Bible willingly did the unthinkable for the greater good? Jael driving a tent peg through Sisera's head. Judith decapitating Holofernes to save her city. Esther breaking royal protocols at the risk of death to save her people.

And maybe the image you're so worried about not meeting was created as a means of control. If you're focused on how you appear to other people, you won't have time to see the more important picture and, perhaps, challenge it."

The silence stretched as Dawna let Felicity's words sink in. Felicity could see her struggle with moving outside the safe role she had adhered to most of her life.

"Dawna, be the woman the angels can respect."

Epilogue

Evan was surprised when he came into the deli for dinner. The tables had been pushed together to form a larger one and an array of food covered the counter.

"It's serve yourself tonight," Ophelia called out as she stacked plates near the cash register.

"We're celebrating Mabon… the autumnal equinox," Jan said in answer to his raised eyebrows. "A kinda last hurrah to the season."

After filling his plate, Evan turned towards his usual table. Becca touched his arm. "Sit with us tonight."

He felt a slight awkwardness as he joined the women at the table. Ophelia offered a prayer for balance in their lives. It was different from the ones that Evan had grown up with but, oddly, it felt right.

"Speaking of balance, I had a chance to see Bethany at the post office today," Felicity said. "Apparently Caleb has officially retired from the church and is going to go back to serving as a fill-in pastor and Dawna is shaking everything to the ground. Bethany said every time a congregant shows up to complain about the new direction, Dawna puts them in charge of improving some aspect of the church for the benefit of the whole congregation. Bethany says she just wishes they hadn't wasted the last thirty-plus years on Caleb."

Ophelia nodded. "Yup, she's not only going to be a great asset for the church, but eventually the community. At least that's what the charts say."

"Have you done our next quarter's chart?" Jan asked.

Her mouth full, Ophelia mmm-hmmmed.

Becca looked at her sharply. "If it doesn't contain unicorns, I don't want to hear what it says. Your last casting sucked big time."

Ophelia glanced around the table as the three other women eyed her warily. She grinned back at them. "Let's just say it's going to be interesting!"

Author Bio

L. Lee Shaw is a teller of tales exploring the vagaries of the human condition. She is the author of five previous novels including the award-winning *Aging Out*. Working from an old farmhouse perched on the side of the Cascade foothills in Oregon, she also runs a tiny publishing business, and has never met a craft she didn't want to try.

Acknowledgements

After hunkering down for an extended period wrestling words onto pages, the time comes when you have to hand them off to others to determine their value. This was the job of my amazing team of beta readers. The first is always my husband, Andrew, who has no qualms about giving me honest feedback. Then comes my faithful friends whose wisdom sharpens the prose and eliminates blunders: Yael Able, Dannie Aastad, Velma Marshall (who writes under the pen name of Amanda Morgan), Carrol Haushalter, and Linda Brewster Rodgers.

However, Mitzee Shaw demands the most credit as he believes the draping of a kitty body over the keyboard while I type is the real source of any inspiration that may strike.

www.ingramcontent.com/pod-product-compliance
Lightning Source LLC
Chambersburg PA
CBHW010547100726
47902CB00008B/2112